EXPOSING THE HEIRESS
Once A Marine Series

JENNIFER
APODACA

Entangled Publishing, LLC
2614 South Timberline Road
Suite 109
Fort Collins, CO 80525
Visit our website at www.entangledpublishing.com.

Ignite is an imprint of Entangled Publishing, LLC.

Edited by Alethea Spiridon Hopson
Cover design by L.J. Anderson
Cover art by Dollar Photo Club

Manufactured in the United States of America

First Edition August 2015

ignite

Chapter One

"The dressing team is here."

Alyssa Brooks dragged her gaze from the computer screen to her administrative assistant. "Already? But..." She glanced at the clock on the computer screen. Four p.m. "Crap."

"You have drinks with executives from Glitterstone Entertainment at six thirty. The team needs to get started on your hair and makeup. There are four outfits to choose from."

She took a deep breath, closing the video she'd been working on.

"Alyssa?" Concern shifted Maxine Lord's voice from efficient assistant to college friend. Shutting the door, the other woman crossed the massive office and perched on her desk. "Spill it. What's wrong?"

"I can't do it." Not another night of playing the role of sophisticated, glamorous, and famous heiress who opened doors and wallets. Her stepfather and fiancé trotted her out as Hollywood royalty, the daughter of the beautiful and talented Jenna Brooks, the actress-turned-screenwriter-turned-business tycoon whose life was tragically cut short.

"Do what?" Maxine asked. "Dinner tonight? Or marry that shark in the designer suit next month?" She leaned on her palm, studying Alyssa. "You're miserable. Why the hell don't you put a stop to all this?"

Because her two best friends, *Guilt* and *Remorse,* wouldn't let her. "Don't start. I'm marrying Nate."

"Do you love him?"

Her thoughts slid back to her first love. Involuntarily, she looked at one of her many framed photographs on her office wall. This one showed strong male hands sculpting a stunning figure of a soldier sharing his meal with a stray dog. For a second all her unhappiness slid away into the memory of summers spent at her friend Erin's house, located on a vineyard in Sonoma, California.

The man in that picture was Hunter Reece, her friend's older brother, home on leave from the Marines. By then, Alyssa had known Hunt for years, but that was the summer she'd fallen head over heels into her inaugural crush. Of course, he'd treated Alyssa like his little sister. Her love had been silent and unrequited. She'd just been his little sister's friend that spent summers with them, nothing more.

"You're doing it again. Staring at the damn picture. Girl, why don't you just look him up?"

"Remind me not to drink with you anymore." She foolishly had too much to drink one night in college and told Maxine how much she'd loved Hunt. Alyssa had spilled her guts…except for her secret, the one she'd told no one but her fiancé.

"You don't love Shark-Nate-O, Alyssa. You deserve

someone who makes you feel like Hunt did."

Even Maxine's nickname for Nate couldn't make her smile. Instead, she shook her head. Hunt was a memory, but he'd hate what she was now. His family had been the most authentic people she knew, while Alyssa had become a stand-in for her mother. She wanted to escape, but her guilt held her as surely as any chains.

At least marrying Nate would give her a chance to have a child. They had a deal—once she got pregnant, she could cut back on all the appearances, photo shoots, dinners, flying all over the world to be seen…pretending to run a company she had very little actual control of.

"What I felt for Hunt was teenaged fantasy. I'm marrying Nate." The tension in her head tightened to pain. "But I'm canceling tonight. I have a headache."

"Are you really sick? Why don't you go home? I'll let Nate know you're not going."

"No!" That was all she needed, another forty-five-minute rant from Nate on how she should fire Maxine, that she didn't know her place, that an employee should not be Alyssa's maid of honor. Then he'd get started on the birthday party Alyssa was hosting for Maxine…

Just thinking about it made her headache worse. "I'll talk to him on my way out." She gathered her purse and she quickly made her way across the hall.

You don't love Nate.

They would grow to love each other, it was just all the stress of the wedding gnawing at both of them. After entering Nate's outer office, she paused by the empty desk of his administrative assistant to compose herself.

Stop stalling, go in there and talk to Nate. Her stomach

tensed, knowing she'd get that disappointed look and the speech about so many people depending on her to do her part. They employed hundreds, and keeping a company this size running in the entertainment industry took networking. That meant keeping the face of Dragon Wing—Alyssa—in all the right places.

Was she being selfish? The spoiled, entitled rich girl?

She lifted her chin. Missing one drinks-and-dinner event was not selfish. Determined, she started toward the door when voices from inside Nate's office caught her attention.

"Everything is set for the wedding. When will the money be in my account?"

Alyssa paused, unsure if she should intrude. Who was Nate talking to?

"One million will be there the day of the wedding."

That was her stepfather Parker Dean's voice. What money were they talking about? What did it have to do with the wedding? Unease gripped her muscles. Alyssa was paying for everything, so what was this about?

"You'll get an additional million each year until we sell the company," Parker said. "Once we pull this off, we'll secure a deal that will make us wealthy enough to shut up any doubters in this town."

Confusion fogged her brain. What was this? Sell Dragon Wing? What did all this have to do with her and Nate marrying? Alyssa backed up a step and dropped a hand down on the desk to steady herself. She had to be misunderstanding this.

"I told you when I approached you to hire me two years ago I could make this work. Between all the reality TV programming and turning Alyssa and me into Hollywood's newest power couple, the company is raking in the money. The big production companies like Glitterstone are taking notice. Another year, maybe two, and we'll sell Dragon Wing for more money than anyone thought possible."

"Just don't get her pregnant for at least a few years. Alyssa is the key and she has to stay visible. But if she gets knocked up, she'll bail on the company, and no amount of guilt or threats will change her mind."

What? The whole point of marrying Nate was so Alyssa could have a family. The one thing she wanted, craved. This couldn't be happening. Nate wouldn't do that. *He knew.* Nate knew how much this meant to her, and why, more than anyone else in the world.

"Not a chance of that."

Nate's cultured voice held the barest trace of a sneer. Sick dread stacked up in her stomach. This wasn't the man she knew, the one who made plans with her for their children. Alyssa would become a silent partner in Dragon Wing, making an occasional appearance as Nate's wife, but her focus would be on their children and developing her little website, Streets of Valor, to showcase her pictures and videos.

"Be sure, an accident—"

"Won't happen," Nate said. "I had a vasectomy years ago."

Buzzing filled her ears and her heart pounded viciously as the word *vasectomy* screamed in her head. Betrayal burned in her throat. She'd thought she'd known her fiancé, a hard-working, ambitious man who'd put himself through law school and climbed the corporate ladder. Parker had noticed his work and hired him as the vice president of business and legal affairs...and apparently to marry and control

Alyssa.

"You did what?" Parker's voice went up a notch. "You never told me that. Does Alyssa know?"

"No and she doesn't need to know. I've worked too hard getting Alyssa to care about me and building our profile to rival Will and Kate and Brad and Angelina. The wedding frenzy is lighting up the internet. I haven't invested this much time and effort to let some kid get in the way."

"If she finds out, this will screw us all. What the hell, Madden? That wasn't part of the deal. She wants kids. I just meant later, not now when we have so much at stake."

A horrible ache spread in her chest. All these years, she'd thought Parker cared about her. Her stepfather was all she had left after her mother died. He was paying Nate to marry her in some *deal* so the two of them could get rich. And Nate... She'd trusted him, thought he'd cared too, that they both wanted the same thing—a family.

All he wanted was her fame and power.

Fool. She was a fool.

"I'll handle Alyssa. She'll do what I want her to."

Rage burst up from her belly, a geyser that spewed for long seconds, as if the top had blown off. And beneath that something else. Something...freeing.

Relief.

The truth was she'd had serious doubts for a couple months, but ignored them. Now she was done. Turning, she started for the door.

Her purse hit the desk, knocking files to the floor.

Crap. She froze, her hands going icy. She didn't want a confrontation, she just wanted to leave and get her head together.

Nate strode out of his office, spotted her, and pulled the door closed. When he turned, his dark eyes met hers. "Why aren't you getting ready for tonight?"

Did he know she'd overheard? Alyssa could confront him now, but her head throbbed too much. She just wanted to get away and think. "I was coming in to tell you I have a headache and won't be going tonight." She crouched down and scooped up the folders.

Handcrafted Italian loafers filled her vision. Nate gripped her elbow, and helped her up. He took the folders and tossed them on the desk. "That's unfortunate."

It took all her will to resist shaking off his hand and stepping back.

"I'll have the limo take you home."

"I drove my car today."

His eyes narrowed. "Why would you do that when we had the dinner this evening?"

Anger exploded. Jerking her arm from his hold, she narrowed her eyes. "Why would you lie to me about wanting children when you've had a vasectomy?" Agony branded her chest. "We made plans together for a family."

His eyes hardened. "I'll have it reversed."

Was he serious? After he'd lied all this time, and had some secret deal with her stepfather to use her? "You think I'd have children with you now? That I'd let you touch me?" Outrage unleashed so much adrenaline her hands trembled.

His long fingers closed around her arm. "You will marry me and continue doing everything I tell you to do."

The hiss in his voice chilled her. Maxine called him a shark, and in this moment, she got it. She pulled her arm from his grasp, she slid off her engagement ring and set it on the desk. "No." She rushed out the door, her heels clicking on the marble. Reaching the elevators in the plush reception area, she fumbled out her card and swiped it. The doors parted silently, in contrast to the fury screaming in her head.

She had to calm down before she drove. Inside the elevator, she took a deep breath just as Nate stormed in, hit the close button, and sealed them inside together.

Alyssa couldn't believe his audacity. "I don't want to see or talk to you."

"Tough." He hit another button and the elevator jerked to a halt. Sudden unease ignited a need to escape. The elevator was too small, and Nate appeared taller. Bigger.

Menacing.

Alyssa lunged toward the control panel.

He caught her hair and shoved her face-first into the mirrored wall. "Listen up, rich girl. I crawled my way out of nothing to real power and a chance at significant wealth. We're marrying and you'll do your part until I say otherwise."

The mirror was cold against her face, but it was his voice against her ear that sent chills down her spine. Nate had never hurt her. Not like this. "You can't—"

"Oh I can and I have. I eliminate problems. Don't be a problem, Alyssa."

"This isn't like you." She tried to get her head around this version of Nate. "You've never threatened me."

Spinning her, he wrapped his hand around her throat. "You never made me. I was perfectly willing to be good to you, even putting up with your no more sex until the wedding nonsense." He leaned in, his dark eyes like onyx stones. "I give you what you want when you give me what I want. Otherwise…you'll pay."

Frantically, she considered her options. She couldn't win a physical battle against him in the elevator. *Be smart. Pacify him until you can get out.* "I see that now."

He released her hair, then hooked an arm around her waist and yanked her against his chest. "Let's make sure you do."

His arm banded her beneath her ribs, making it hard to breathe. Fear pounded in her head. God, he was pushing her around, hurting her.

"You try anything, and I'll start extracting payment here." He held up his phone, the screen filled with a photograph.

Recognition gut-punched her. "You wouldn't. He's just a kid."

"I know exactly where he is, every minute of every day. Play your part, and I'll leave him alone. Fuck me over, and I'll hurt him. Then you."

Bile shot up in her throat. There on the screen was a picture of her son.

The boy she'd given up for adoption seven years ago.

Chapter Two

"You called me in on a babysitting job for a rich heiress?" Hunter Reece dropped his ass down on Sienna Lorrey's desk. "Aren't there some real jobs out there?"

Leaning back in her chair, Sienna shoved her glasses up to the top of her blonde head and eyed him. "This heiress asked for you by name."

Now she had his full attention. "Who is she?"

Si lifted her brow. "Alyssa Brooks."

It took a lot to shock him, but this… "Alyssa?" He couldn't process it. "She asked for me?"

"Specifically."

He narrowed his eyes. "You couldn't tell me this when you called me in?" The last time he'd seen Alyssa had been at her mother's funeral seven years ago. It had torn him up to see her in so much pain. A stark difference from all the years she'd visited the vineyard. Then she'd been young and vibrant, full of piss and vinegar just like his little sister.

Except when Alyssa had her camera in her hand. Then she'd go quiet and focused.

Like Hunt with a gun in his hand.

Christ, talk about a sick comparison. She captured life in her lens, while Hunt had killed with a precision so cold he'd become a legend.

Si swiveled in her chair, regaining his attention. Amusement tugged her lips. "I could have, but then I'd have missed your shocked reaction. Never seen your eyes lose focus like that. How well do you know this woman?"

He'd known the girl, not the polished glamorous woman he saw all over the media. And back then, he'd been a different person. "She was my kid sister's friend. Her mom and my mom were friends, and Alyssa came to stay with us for several summers." So yeah, it'd thrown him a little to hear her name. He connected her with a happier time in his life, but those times were done, and he had a job to do. She'd called Once A Marine Security Agency, so she had to be in some kind of trouble. "What's her story?"

The front door of the office opened and Hunt whipped around, automatically stepping in front of Si to shield her. His attention honed in on the doorway.

"It's a client, not a terrorist." Si's voice bubbled with humor.

Ignoring that comment, something kicked in Hunt's chest as Alyssa walked through the door. The girl he remembered had been filled with vibrant color, but the woman before him sucked his breath from his chest. Her dark hair was pulled back in a simple ponytail, her makeup-free face had carved away childhood roundness to sculpted cheekbones and full lips. Her round eyes were framed in sooty lashes. She wore a casual T-shirt that slid over tantalizing breasts, and jeans that molded to her hips and thighs.

She looked nothing like the glossy photos of her that turned up in the media.

No, this woman walked straight out of his dreams. Every single nerve twanged in reaction. His blood simmered. Hunger gnawed low in his belly, growing with every heartbeat into a shocking pool of need.

Never had this happened. Ever. Oh, he'd had instant lust, but this… What the hell? Lyssie, well Alyssa now, was his little sister's friend. He'd practically seen her grow up. Even with the air of tension and worry riding her, and the dark circles staining the delicate skin under her brown eyes, she was gorgeous. "Alyssa."

Her eyes scanned the office and landed on him. Her mouth curved in a smile he remembered so well, one side tilting up slightly more than the other. "Hunt."

Her voice took him back to those summers, tossing the girls in the pool because it'd made them squeal. Making s'mores with them in the evenings out at the fire pit. It reminded him of a lighter era. But in those days, her voice had never pulled at something low in his guts. Oh, he'd known she was pretty, but she'd been a kid. Now she was a beautiful woman.

"Thank you for agreeing to see me."

Coming to a stop a foot or two away, he resisted the urge to pull her into a hug and shield her from that troubled look dulling the specks of gold in her brown eyes.

Sienna cleared her throat. "Miss Brooks, I'm Sienna Lorrey. We spoke on the phone."

"Nice to meet you. Call me Alyssa."

He focused on his job, not the slew of regrets seeing

Alyssa stirred up. "What brings you here?"

That spark in her eyes died out. She shifted her weight and twisted her fingers together. "I need help."

A warning shot fired in his brain. "What kind of help?"

She glanced around. "Kind of hard to explain."

Only minutes had passed, and already the old feelings of protectiveness he'd developed when she was a kid tangled with a newer more complex reaction. Hoping to put her at ease, he touched her shoulder. "I told you once, if you ever need me, I'd be there."

"You remember that?"

"I don't forget promises." It had been at her mother's funeral, and he'd wanted to scoop her up and take her home where she could finish growing up with his parents and sister to look out for her, since Hunt had to go back to duty in the Marines.

She'd been seventeen then, and her stepfather had been named her guardian. Alyssa seemed okay with that, or as okay as she could be given that she just lost her mom in a tragic accident. But now? Her eyes bled fear which pissed him off. Time to get to work. Laying his hand on her lower back, he glanced at Si. "We'll be in the conference room." He led her to a short hallway, trying to ignore her softness beneath his hard palm and her scent of vanilla and sunshine.

He stopped at the door on his left and tugged his hand back. Gesturing to the oblong table that stretched across the center of the room, he said, "Take any seat you like." After snagging his tablet, he took a place across from her. "Do you need anything before we get started? Water? Coffee?"

She shook her head. "I don't know where to start. And telling you…" She looked up at the ceiling.

"What?"

Alyssa pulled her mouth tight, lowered her chin and faced him. "That summer when I was fourteen, I had a crush on you."

His mouth quirked. "I know." He was a guy, of course he knew, but he'd been twenty then and careful to treat her like his sister. "But that has nothing to do with now." She'd grown up.

"It'd help if you'd gotten fat or were going bald."

That startled a laugh from him. Oh yeah, this was Alyssa. She'd always been funny. "Sorry to disappoint."

"It's okay, I'll deal with it. I'm tough like that."

Was she? Because from where he sat she looked lonely, something he understood all too well. "I heard that you're engaged." He glanced at her finger. No ring.

Alyssa rubbed her thumb over the bare digit. "Not anymore. I took the ring off last night." She leaned forward, folding her hands together on the table. "Right after I discovered that my stepfather is paying Nate Madden to marry me."

"Paying him? Why would he have to pay any man to marry you?" That didn't make any sense. She was gorgeous, rich, and powerful. A thousand questions stacked up in his brain.

Her shoulders sagged. "To keep me doing what I'm doing."

Hunt was trying to follow. "Aren't you running your mother's company?" He had to amend that. "Your company now."

"Not just mine, it belongs to me and Parker, but it's my face, name, and perceived fame that keeps the company growing. I hate it, and both Parker and Nate know it."

"Then why do you do it?"

"In the beginning, I did it for Parker. When my mom

died, it all fell to him. He struggled for the first couple years. People were pulling away, unsure if he could carry the company. Without Jenna Brooks, the trust and faith that are so crucial in entertainment were gone. The company slipped into the red." She sighed. "I couldn't let my mother's company fail so I began doing appearances representing Dragon Wing. By the time I finished college, I had a corner office at Dragon Wing Productions, the name president on my door, and a full itinerary of travel and events."

Hunt leaned back, studying her. What really drove her to stay doing something she didn't like? "So walk away. You're not trapped in a job trying to feed your kids or pay the electric bill."

She flinched. "That was my plan. Marry Nate, have a child, and then I'd fade away to work on my photography, but then I found out that wasn't going to happen either."

There was a sadness about her that was like an itch on his skin. The only time Hunt felt much of anything was during sex or sculpting, but this girl... Something about her was getting to him. "Go on."

"I can't believe how naive, how dumb I was." She shook her head. "Dragon Wing became profitable again and rising. At that point I wanted out, to become a silent partner."

"What stopped you?"

"Nate. Parker hired him as the vice president of business and legal affairs. It started small, Parker would ask me to go with Nate to a cocktail party. Nate would tell me how Parker had invested every last penny into the company, and if we worked together, we could help him succeed. How the company was everything to my stepfather since he'd lost my mom." She bit her lip. "My mom left Parker a few million, but the bulk of her wealth came to me and I felt guilty. Responsible. Mom loved Parker…so I did it. At first, we set up these 'dates' for the media to catch us on. But before I knew it, Nate and I were truly dating."

Warning bells clanged in his head. Alyssa had grown up rich and sheltered, she was whip-smart, but all things considered, it wouldn't be that hard for a skilled manipulator to get control. Hunt had seen it happen over and over.

"Then we started talking about marriage and children, and I fell for it, never realizing my stepfather was paying him as part of some plan the two of them cooked up to keep me on as the face of Dragon Wing." Her eyes narrowed, her nostrils flared. "I overheard Nate the other day tell Parker he'd had a vasectomy years ago."

Talk about underhanded. "Okay, so you broke up with him. What is it you want from me?" It sounded more like she needed a lawyer.

She leveled her gaze on him. "Protection. I've broken off our engagement and quit Dragon Wing. I need to get out of L.A. for a while and I want to hire you as my bodyguard."

A buzz of fury lit up his veins. "Has Nate ever hurt you? Are you afraid of him?" She must be if she wanted to leave town.

Her eyes clouded. "Not until last night. He shoved me in the elevator, and told me I will marry him and made threats. Not just against me, but also…" She sucked in her lips, angry color splashing over her cheeks.

Hunt fisted his hands as adrenaline powered into his veins. What had the bastard done to her? He didn't see any marks. But —

"He threatened my son."

Chapter Three

"You have a kid?"

Alyssa immediately looked around, her compelling need to keep the boy safe and protected rising to the surface. All these years, she'd only told one person about him. But what did she expect—paparazzi to leap out from behind a hidden wall and hear this amazing scoop that Alyssa Brooks had a child and kept it secret? She took a breath and looked at the man across from her.

Hunt. The years had carved away all traces of the boy into a hard man. His sandy-colored hair was longer than the military-short cut she'd last seen him with. But the careless, finger-combed length did nothing to soften the hard angles of his face, or the frost in his light blue eyes. She dragged her gaze over his shoulders straining the material of his T-shirt, and the muscles and tendons bulging along his biceps...and oh, there was beautiful script flowing out from the arm of his shirt.

"Alyssa."

He snapped out her name like a command, yanking her stare up. "Not anymore." *Tell him.* "I gave him up for adoption the day he was born." Just saying the words swept her back seven years to that morning in the cold hospital room. She had held her newborn son in her arms and felt her heart breaking crack by painful crack.

She hadn't wanted to give him up, but she'd loved him too much to saddle him with a teenaged, grief-and-guilt-ridden mother. Beneath the conference table, Alyssa pressed her fist into her belly over the small heart and tear tattoo she had there. The silence grew so thick it was hard to breathe. "His parents know I'm arranging protection for him, well for all of them."

"You're hiring us to protect a baby you didn't want?"

His voice shot down that tiny hope in her that he'd understand. Support her. That she wouldn't feel so damned alone and scared. "Nate threatened to hurt me and Eli." At Hunt's confused expression, she said, "Eli is the name his adopted parents gave him, and I'm willing to pay anything to keep Eli and his parents safe." She'd sacrificed part of her heart to give that boy a good life. "Disapprove of me all you want, but that boy is only seven years old."

"Seven. That would have made you seventeen when you had him."

Where was he going with this? "Yes."

"So when your mom died…"

God. She didn't want to go back to those memories. "I was two months pregnant."

Something flickered in his eyes, a streak of sympathy maybe? Or was she just reaching?

"Oh, hell, Lyssie." His old nickname for her slipped out. "Why didn't you tell my mom? Or Erin. My sister was your best friend and you cut her out."

Tell them? She'd been in total shock from the accident that killed her mom. Gritting her teeth, she said, "None of that matters now. What is important is that Eli's safe." She repeated everything Nate had said, his ultimatum that she marry him, and ended with his final threat after showing her the picture of her son. "I know exactly where he is, every minute of every day. Play your part, and I'll leave him alone. Fuck me over, and I'll hurt him. Then you." Taking a breath, she added, "I don't want to go to the police. Nate will just deny that he made a threat. And once I make a police report about Eli's existence, the media could pick it up and that would open a whole can of worms." Looking Hunt in the eyes, she asked, "Will Once A Marine take on the case or not?" And if they didn't, then what?

"I have a few questions."

Fighting a wave of impatience, she nodded.

"Does your stepfather know you had a baby?"

She shook her head. "No. I was afraid he'd make me have an abortion, and he was too wrapped up in trying to save Dragon Wing to notice. Although Nate may have told him by now."

"Then how'd you give the baby up with no one knowing?"

Focus on the details, not the painful memories. "Our longtime housekeeper, Carmen, figured out I was pregnant and took me to Arizona where we stayed with her family. Carmen told Parker she was getting me away from the media attention that wouldn't let up after the accident and my mom's death. He was glad to have me gone and never realized there was more to it."

He typed something into his iPad. "You gave him up in Arizona?"

It was all a blur—until he was born. Those hours were vivid. "Yes, I hired a private adoption attorney, and through her found the couple, Mark and Janis. We screened a lot of people, but they were perfect."

"Did the kid's father agree to the adoption? Or did you even tell him?"

Alyssa studied the mahogany table. "I told him. He came over to break up with me because he was leaving on tour. He was in a boy band. His name is Scott Pierson. He was upset and wanted me to get rid of it." She fisted her hands. "Anyway, he signed the papers and I haven't talked to him since then. He doesn't even know who adopted Eli."

Long beats of silence passed. "Did you tell Nate where the boy is?"

The fear she'd lived with all night burned in her gut. "No, I only told him that I had Eli and gave him up after he asked me to marry him. Eli's in my will, so Nate had to know. I never told him where Eli and his parents are now, but he obviously found out. I saw the picture of him."

"Which is where? Are you sure it was Eli?"

She couldn't hold Hunt's gaze and stared over his shoulder at the gray wall. "He's in Scottsdale, Arizona. I get pictures and an email once a year, no other contact unless there is a problem." She swallowed. "It's him. I know his face better than my own. Nothing matters more than protecting Eli and his family. Nate has someone watching the family, and we need to find out who and make it stop. Nate left this morning for Europe for a week. I'm hoping that gives us a

little time before he does something truly awful." Alyssa dug
her fingers into her palms as her desperation rose. "Will you
help me? Keep Eli and me safe?"

He pushed the iPad aside and stacked his hands. "Your
ex fiancé is using the son you love to blackmail you into
marrying him, and that kind of shit really pisses me off. We'll
get a team on Eli and his family."

"Thank you, that makes me feel better about Eli."
Alyssa admitted that she was scared for herself too. "But
what about me? Will you be my bodyguard?"

· · ·

Hunt got up and rounded the table, pulled to the girl he'd
never forgotten. He was still reeling that she'd had a baby.
And had then given him up.

When he'd come home from the Marines, he'd seen
Alyssa on TV and thought she'd taken to the rich and powerful life, leaving the remnants of her other life behind, that
she'd forgotten them.

But now? She took his breath away. A young woman
who fought this hard to protect the child she hadn't seen in
seven years, other than in pictures, wasn't shallow and vain.
This woman touched places in him best left alone.

No way would he let someone else protect her. Dropping
into the chair next to her, he took in the dark shadows under
her eyes. "Did you sleep at all last night?"

"No. I was too worried and was trying to figure out what
to do."

In her desperation she'd come to him. That sealed his
decision. "You were my little sister's best friend. You're not

a job and I'm not taking money to protect you." Unable to resist, he touched her shoulder. That contact zinged through him, sending sparks into the cold darkness he'd been living in for years. "Instead, I'm taking you home to Sonoma. I installed the security system, and you'll be safe there."

Hope lit up her eyes. "The vineyard? Wait, maybe your parents won't want me there. If anyone finds out I'm there, the place will be swarmed with reporters."

This was what she had lived all these years. "I own the place now. My parents stay there when they want to, but right now, they're in Scotland."

Her expression softened. "There's no place else I'd rather go."

In that second, with Lyssie looking at him like he was her own personal hero, he knew he was in trouble. No, he could do this. He'd treat her like he always had.

Like a kid sister.

• • •

Alyssa caught her breath as they drove through the wrought iron gates into the small vineyard.

It was like coming home. A sensation so powerful, her eyes burned and her chest ached. Here she'd been happy. Oh, she'd been happy with her mom too, but here in Sonoma, the stress and pressures of her mom's fame never touched them. Even when Jenna came to visit Alyssa on weekends during the summers, the press didn't bother them. Both her mother and Alyssa could just be themselves.

Blinking away the sheen of tears, she took in the sinking sun casting a golden orange light over the green vines lining the narrow road. Unable to resist, she rolled down her window. The damp air carried a sweet, slightly citrusy and sensual fragrance. "Do you still sell the grapes to wineries?"

"Yep."

They crested a hill and the one-story Mediterranean house came into view, looking very much as she remembered it. Once he parked, she jumped out and headed to the bottom of the stairs to touch the whale sculpture rising out of a left pillar. At the top and on the right was a lion guarding the terrace. Alyssa couldn't resist tracing the details of the creature's mane.

"It's not alive. It's stone." Hunt smirked at her as he carried the bags past her.

"Ha ha. Don't be mean. You get to see these whenever you want. Your dad's amazing at carving stone into shapes that look so real." She took in the gray flagstone terrace lined with low palm trees and flowers, then she rotated and *holy crap,* the stunning vision of gently rolling hills covered in vines captured her.

"Surveying your kingdom, princess?"

She flushed at the memory. She and Erin had been playing princesses trapped in a castle dungeon, and they needed a prince to rescue them. Alyssa tried to get Hunt to play the role. He'd refused as any twelve-year-old boy would. Mad and pretty much used to getting her way, she'd said, *I'm Princess Alyssa, you have to do what I say.*

He'd laughed in her face and told her he wasn't going to be some dumb prince, he was going to be a Marine. Calling her princess became one of his teasing nicknames.

"Joke's on you, Marine. You're rescuing me."

Hunt laughed. "You got your wish. I'm playing your

hero now."

He'd moved so close behind her that his words feathered over her exposed neck. Her skin prickled with sudden awareness of his size and heat. Even as a little girl, she'd wanted him for her hero, but she wasn't a child anymore and this wasn't a game. Embarrassed at her intense reaction to his nearness—to him—she wrapped her arms around her waist. She'd expected some nostalgia at seeing Hunt again. But this was vastly different from when she'd been six and wanted to play a game. Or fourteen and fell so hard for him, wondering what it'd be like if he held her hand with his strong artist's fingers. Or if he kissed her.

She wasn't a girl anymore. No, she was a scared woman who'd foolishly trusted the wrong man. At least she knew Eli was safe for now. One of the Once A Marine guys, Griff Rankin, was already there, and had sent Hunt a text that the family was secure. She needed to unravel the mess she was in, not add more complications.

She slipped to the side and reached for her bag. "I guess we should get settled."

Hunt tugged the bag from her hand and headed into the house, stopping to key in a code on an alarm pad.

Alyssa glanced in the earth-toned living room on the right and office on the left, before going into a great room. On the left was the kitchen. Thick crockery dishes in glass-fronted cabinets and marble counters with rich earthy veins proved some updating had been done. In the center of the room stood a long table made of reclaimed wood on a scroll iron base. And the right had a corner couch covered in throw pillows and facing a big screen TV. That sense of familiarity swept over her. Oh, sure, the countertops, couch and a few other things had changed, but overall the house still had that same homey feel.

He led her past the sitting area to the hallway. After entering the first door on the left, he set her suitcase on the thick white comforter piled high with burgundy pillows. Her room. The one she had every summer she'd stayed there from the time she'd started coming right after her dad died. Alyssa had been barely six. Her mom had to work long hours and wanted Alyssa to have fun on her summer breaks without constant bodyguards. She and Erin had bonded and it just seemed like a good solution. Plus her mom came on weekends and she got to relax too.

With too many emotions swimming through her, she focused on Hunt. He took up a lot of space in the room. Had she forgotten how tall he was—passing the six foot mark while she hovered around five and a half feet? When she'd been really young, he'd seemed huge and massively strong to her. He could pick her up and toss her in the air.

He still looked as if he could easily pick her up or handle almost anything life threw his way. Strength and confidence flowed from him in a steady stream, along with an undercurrent of danger.

The need to understand this man drew her attention to the script wrapped in tribal markings flowing over his biceps. Moving closer, she tried to read it but part of it was hidden beneath the arm of his T-shirt. "What does this script say?" Giving into impulse, she traced one of the lines.

He sucked in his breath.

She jerked her fingers back. She'd been stroking his skin, as fascinated by the hills and valleys of his muscles as the beautiful markings. What was wrong with her?

Hunt shoved up his shirt sleeve and turned to show her. "Brothers in blood."

That meant something to him important enough to mark his skin, just like her tat did to her, and she wanted to grasp it. Since he only had a sister, she asked, "For the men you served with?"

"Yes. I'd bleed for them." He rotated and pushed up the other sleeve, showing her his left arm. "This is for all the ones who gave their lives."

Leaning closer, she studied the ink. "Sacrifice Remembered." That powered through her, the absolute and permanent respect he gave the men who died serving their country. Lifting her eyes, she said, "Last time I saw you, you didn't have any tats."

Dropping his sleeve, he studied her. "I'm not that guy anymore."

No he wasn't. That idealistic young man with the ready smile and laughing eyes had hardened into this powerful, sexy, and shrouded in darkness man, one that tugged at a part of her that had been numb for seven years.

She could see he was somehow warning her, but of what? Besides, she'd changed too. "I'm not that girl who had the silly crush on you."

Hunt's gaze cleared and a grin tugged at the corners of his mouth. "Nope, you don't get to make it unimportant. I was your first crush, wasn't I?"

Whoa, that was a quick change from dark to playful. She went with it and waved a hand at him. "Please, I was an impressionable girl with a new crush every other day."

He lifted an eyebrow. "You're making that up. Take it back."

That familiar teasing glint in Hunt's eyes eased the knot of tension that had been lodged between her shoulder blades since yesterday. "Nope, totally true. I think you were like the fifth guy that summer that I had a tiny crush on."

"Tiny?" He crossed his arms, his shoulders bulging beneath his T-shirt as he glared at her with a challenge. "That's cruel, baby girl. I was your first big crush. Admit it."

Hearing another of his old nicknames for her stirred warmth deep in her chest. Hunt hadn't ever had romantic feelings about her, but he'd cared. And he still cared enough to bring her back to the vineyard now and help her. His friendship meant everything to her. But she wanted to keep things light, easy. "Do you get tired from carting around that oversized ego?"

"Look who's talking about ego, cover girl. I can't buy a damn candy bar without you staring at me in the checkout line."

She rolled her eyes. "That's not me. Aside from the long list of talented people doing my hair, makeup, nails, clothes and jewelry, those pictures are airbrushed. There's nothing real there."

Hunt shuddered. "No wonder you wanted to escape. All those people buzzing around would irritate the shit out of me."

A laugh bubbled up her throat. "It's annoying, but I have to be nice. That's exhausting." And so useless. It'd be different if being a model was what she wanted to do. But Alyssa was famous for nothing more than being her mother's daughter, and having been in the accident that killed Jenna Brooks—the famous child actress turned screenwriter and producer. That one horrible night had left the public with an insatiable curiosity about Alyssa and she hated it.

"Well, now that you've made your escape, why don't you get settled? I'll call in a pizza." He headed out and paused in the doorway, his eyes cautious. "Do you still eat pizza?"

She smiled. "Only if my personal chef makes it."

Hunt's jaw dropped.

Alyssa rolled her eyes. "Kidding. Yes, I still eat pizza. Sheesh."

A gleam lit up his eyes. "Once I'd have picked you up and tossed you in the pool for yanking my chain like that."

Echoes of her and Erin's screaming laughter when Hunt or his dad had done that played in her mind. "Sure, but you were young then. Now you're like what? Thirty? You'd probably throw out your back."

Hunt strode across the hall, tossed his bag in his room, and turned to lean a shoulder against the doorjamb. "Are you baiting me? That water's cold. I haven't started the heater yet."

She laughed. "Let's call it payback for thinking I'm such a snob."

"Now that we have your food preferences cleared up, you must be hungry. You just picked at your food when we stopped for lunch."

She should have realized he'd noticed that. Since last night, she'd been too upset to eat. "Nerves I guess."

"Yeah?" Hunt crossed the hallway and loomed over her. "How are you feeling now?"

Easy answer. "Safe." Something she hadn't felt in a long time.

Chapter Four

After her shower, she followed her nose out to the family room. The scents wafting from the closed pizza box resting on the island made her stomach rumble.

Hunt had his back to her as he opened a bottle of wine. The ends of his damp hair hit about mid-neck. A white T-shirt pulled across his back as he expertly uncorked the wine. He wore black pajama bottoms… *Stop*. She pulled her eyes up just as he turned.

His gaze tangled with hers, then rolled over her gray racer back tank and leggings, practically scorching them off her skin.

Alyssa's breath caught at the naked approval in his eyes. Then he blinked and blanked the expression. "Griff checked in while you were in the shower. Everything is fine. He has a team coming in tomorrow. The kid is safe."

It took everything she had not to ask the questions blaring in her mind. *How does Eli look? Has his front tooth grown in yet? Is he happy?* Alyssa had the yearly pictures but that was like getting two drops of water after being stranded in the desert for years. She craved more. And it infuriated her that Nate had pictures—at least the one he'd shown her, but probably more.

"Okay, thanks."

"I wondered if you'd ask for more pictures than you already get, or grill Griff about the kid."

She shook her head. "No. I mean I want it, but I have an agreement with his parents. They are in control of what pictures and information I get about Eli. And they're being extremely cooperative about me providing protection. I won't overstep that." No matter how much she wanted to. She'd given up the right, pure and simple. Now she had to live with that choice.

"Fair enough." He held up the bottle. "Wine?"

Bad idea. She was tired, hungry, and too vulnerable. She opened her mouth to say no. "Sure." Huh, there seemed to be a miscommunication between her brain and tongue.

"Can you grab a couple waters from the fridge? I started the fire pit in the front. Let's eat there."

They went outside and settled around the stone pit in the center of the terrace. The dark, grape-scented night and gently crackling flames soothed some of her ragged edges. Propping her feet up on the stone ring, she took the plate piled with pizza. The smell tantalized her again, finally tripping her memory. Her mouth watered, but she turned to Hunt who sat next to her. "Greek pizza?"

"It was your favorite."

Her heart did a happy little skip that he remembered. "I haven't had this in years." She took a huge bite, her mouth filling with the feta cheese, peppers and olives. "Better than I remember."

The wine warmed her along with the fire as she stuffed herself with pizza. Curiosity that she'd been suppressing all day surfaced. "So you bought this place from your parents?" It couldn't be cheap.

"Yep, right when I came home two years ago. They were tired of the upkeep and wanted to travel. Both Erin and I didn't want to let it go, but she's not in a financial position to buy it, so I did."

Every time he mentioned his sister, Alyssa missed her more. "Erin's Loft is doing well. I follow her online." Erin sold the products of local artists, including her own pottery.

"Yes, but her business takes a lot of her money, and I didn't want her getting in over her head. And…"

"What?" She turned, watching him in the firelight.

"I needed a place to sculpt."

"Oh." There was an intensity beneath that statement she didn't understand. Hunt's parents and sister were driven art-ists—his mom painted, his dad carved stone, and Erin did pottery. For Hunt, it had been more of a hobby. He had an insane amount of talent, but his love had been the military. So when had this need manifested itself? "Is the studio still out back?"

Hunt's jaw twitched, then he turned. "I keep it locked. You can go anywhere else in or out of the house, feel free to use the pool, whatever you want. But the studio is off-limits."

She lowered her slice of pizza, her stomach tensing. Years ago, she would burst into the studio when he was working, and he never cared. Had welcomed her. She'd take pictures or chatter, but mostly she'd just wanted to sit there, letting the music he had playing wash over her as she watched him sculpt. And now he didn't want her in there.

She opened her mouth to ask why, then thought better of it. She hadn't seen him or his family in years; she didn't have the right to demand answers. He'd been extraordinarily generous to bring her here, keep her safe, arrange for protection of Eli and his family. For the first time in the last miserable twenty-four hours she felt safe. If he wanted her to stay out of his studio, then she'd respect that. "Okay."

"I don't let anyone in there, it's not just you."

There it was again, that tension eating at him. She reached across the space separating them and touched his forearm. "I'll respect your privacy."

He relaxed, grabbing another slice of pizza.

"So what are your folks doing in Scotland? Sightseeing?" She smiled thinking of them.

"Mom has a job there. One of her former art students became a bestselling author, bought an old castle ruins and built a house on the property. Mom is painting a few murals in the house."

"Castle ruins?" Alyssa was instantly caught up in the romance of it. "Is it authentic? My mom told me stories of her and my dad going to Scotland to tour some of the ruins. I've always wanted to go, maybe take some pictures."

Hunt topped off her wine glass. "Why haven't you done it?"

Who would she have gone with? She hadn't taken a real vacation in years. "No time. My travel is all booked by Dragon Wing for work. The Cannes Film Festival. Monaco. Or locations for promoting reality TV shows or made-for-TV movies. Anyway, I'll go one day." She sipped some wine and changed the subject. "I bet the murals your mom's painting are amazing."

"You could visit my parents and see them. The owner isn't there, and they'll be there for another few weeks until they need to be back for the award dinner."

"They're getting an award?"

"Lifetime achievement award from P.A.L. for more than thirty years of supporting peace over violence. It's at a hotel in L.A."

"Wow, honored by the Peace Advancement League, that's wonderful." His parents were dedicated pacifists, so very different from Hunt. Yet they hadn't tried to stop Hunt from following his dreams as far as Alyssa knew.

"I'm sure they'd love you to come to the award dinner."

"Maybe." First she had to sort out her life. "Right now, this is perfect. Just sitting here with the fire pit going, great pizza and wine." She took another sip, enjoying the peaceful night. "So what about you, Hunt? You're obviously not married unless you're hiding your wife in the locked art studio." Hmm, the wine was loosening her tongue.

"That sounds like a movie plot, cover girl."

She glared at him. "Really? Calling me cover girl is going to be a thing now?"

"Does it bug you?"

"Yes."

"Then it's going to be a thing."

Of course it was. She walked right into that by admitting it bugged her. Wait…he'd evaded her question. "So no wife then. Are you dating?" He wasn't planning on being here alone forever right? The vineyard was meant to be lived in. Maybe a couple dogs chasing squirrels or stretched out by the fire…and yep, she'd had enough wine. Alyssa set her glass down. "I'm waiting for an answer."

"No."

The abruptness startled her. "No you won't answer or no you aren't dating?"

Orange and yellow light danced over the profile of his face. Tension rode his jaw, and she had to reclaim her wine glass to keep from tracing it, or sinking her fingers into his hair. Was he going to answer her? "Hunt?"

"I don't date."

"Ever?"

"Not in nearly two years."

"So maybe it's not weird that I stopped wanting sex with Nate two months ago—" *Stop talking.* Alyssa slapped her hand over her mouth, a flush heating her neck and cheeks. Squeezing her eyes shut, she spread her fingers and said, "Let's forget I said that. Stupid wine."

"I would, except you accused me of having a wife locked up in my studio. So…payback sucks, baby girl. You're telling me that a living, breathing man agreed to stop having sex with a beautiful woman like you?"

"What about you? You don't date, so obviously you're not big on sex." Were they actually talking about this?

"I said I don't date, as in having a relationship. I never said I don't have sex. I'm a huge fan of sex. It's right up there in my top five favorite things."

Alyssa couldn't tear her gaze from him as the firelight played over the hard edges of him. Once he'd been the poster boy for clean-cut military, now he'd gone all tatted up sexy danger.

"Your turn. Why were you going to marry a man you

stopped wanting?"

She didn't know how to answer that. Had she really ever wanted Nate, or was sex expected of her and so she did it? "Sex got to be too much work."

"Sex is work?"

"Nate was attracted to the woman on the magazine covers. Full makeup, sexy but not slutty lingerie." And she was telling Hunt this why? *Because you could always talk to him.* "After a while sex was as much work as getting ready for a photo shoot or appearance. And frankly, the payoff wasn't that great."

Hunt choked on his wine, his head jerking up and eyes colliding with hers.

The fire crackled. At least it better be the fire and not the tension tightening low in her belly. Why did his perusal make her vividly aware of her body, of herself?

"I don't know what the hell you were doing, Lyssie, but that wasn't sex. Not the kind you deserve with a man who cares about your pleasure. There's nothing hotter than a woman losing control from my touch. Nothing. Not a perfect body, lingerie, makeup or anything can compare to watching her eyes lose focus, her body shudder from bliss... That's sexy and it's a gift. But you know what really pisses me off?"

She leaned over the arm of her chair, drawn to him, to the force of Hunt and his words. "What?"

"You didn't care either. You let a man treat you that way, and that's not okay, Lyssie."

Confusion tangled with the power of his statement. Old guilt reminded her that she'd been selfish too many times with terrible consequences. "I let him because I wanted a baby, and I wanted it to be right this time. Married, secure, the child loved and shielded. I thought Nate wanted that too. Instead, I just made another mistake, another bad decision that led to painful consequences." It took an effort to meet his scrutiny.

"What other bad decisions are you talking about?"

"I had unprotected sex and got pregnant." The memories pressed in on her, stealing her breath. Getting up, she reached for her plate.

Hunt caught her wrist in a gentle grip. "One mistake. We all make them."

He needed to know the truth. "Maybe, but not everyone's mistakes end in a crash that kills their mother." She tugged her wrist free and headed inside.

• • •

Hunt gripped the arms of the chair to keep himself from going after her. Shit. All these years, she'd been carrying that? He narrowed his eyes on the fire, his instincts screaming. He'd wondered how her stepfather, and later her fiancé, controlled her. Now it made a sick kind of sense.

The front door opened and Lyssie returned, stopping by her chair. Her eyes brimmed with uncertainty and pain, then firmed into determination. "Eli wasn't a mistake. I mean getting pregnant was careless and foolish, but a child is not a mistake." She pivoted on her bare foot and took a step.

Goddamn. That right there grabbed him by the throat. She cared so much for the baby she gave up and he respected that. He shot up and caught her hand. "Lyssie, don't go." He eased her down into the chair, then settled into his own.

She faced him. "I couldn't let you believe I think he's a

mistake."

"But it's okay if I believe your actions led to your mother's death?"

She pulled her knees up and locked her arms around her legs. "I never told anyone else this, not even the police, but that night, I told my mom I was pregnant. That's why the two of us were at the restaurant. I thought if we were out at dinner, she'd take the news better." She tilted her head back, gazing up. Taking a deep breath, she said, "I never saw that look on her face before. Such disappointment. Then she got a migraine and was really sick."

Hunt stayed quiet, just letting her talk.

"We left, but reporters swarmed us as we walked out of the restaurant. They'd heard that Scott had broken up with me to go on tour with his band. They wanted to know how it felt to be dumped by him. My mom tried to pull me back inside to call our bodyguard to come get us instead, but I insisted I could drive us home." She lowered her chin to her knees. "Parker told me I should have listened to my mother. He could barely look at me that first year after the accident. The truth is, when Carmen took me away to Arizona, he was relieved."

That bastard had twisted Alyssa's misgivings, those *what ifs* everyone asks themselves after a tragedy, into deep remorse then used that to control her. What she'd needed was love and maybe some counseling to help her cope. Hunt had seen the police report—it was shown by the media every year on the anniversary of Jenna Brook's death. The accident had been the result of a torrential downpour on a treacherous road. Of course, the press highlighted the part about an inexperienced driver—Alyssa—being stated as a contributing factor. Anger drove spikes into his gut. "You didn't know what would happen. You can't blame yourself when you didn't know."

Alyssa shivered. "By the time we got in the car, Mom was even sicker." She shut her eyes in memory. "Why didn't I check?"

Self-hatred weighed down her words. "Check what?"

She wrapped her arms tighter. "Her seat belt. I put mine on, but never checked hers. She hadn't put it on. When we hit the tree, she was thrown in the car and the head trauma killed her."

That had been in the accident report too, but it was her guilt and pain that roused his compulsion to comfort her. *Don't do it.* But his need outweighed common sense. Getting up, he caught her hands and pulled her to her feet.

She tilted her head up. "What?"

The loneliness mixed with remorse in her eyes cut him with an all too familiar knife. His self-preservation warned, *Don't do this. Keep your distance*, but he couldn't fight the need to care for her. "You're cold and upset, and I don't like it. Come here." He sat and tugged her down onto his lap. She filled his arms with a weight that stirred a longing for more. So much more. Things he couldn't have.

"You don't have to do this."

"Yeah, I do." No one had protected her. Hunt had left the day after her mother's funeral to go back to duty. His mom and Erin went home to their lives and they left her at the mercy of her stepfather.

She'd been young, stricken with guilt and grief, and pregnant. She'd needed someone to stand for her until she was strong enough to stand for herself. And he'd had the gall, the utter nerve, to tell her that it wasn't okay that she'd let her ex not care for her pleasure. No one had taught her that she was worthy and that was changing now. This wasn't about sex, it was about showing her that she was a woman of worth.

"Why?"

Considering that, he asked, "Remember that first day your mom brought you here for the summer? You were six, I think, and carrying that stuffed dog."

Her eyes softened. "My dad gave him to me. After he died, I carried him everywhere for a year." A smile ghosted her lips. "I still have him."

That sounded like her, so sentimental. "I'd broken my arm the day before you got here. The plan had been for me to go on my dad's rock sculpting job to Australia for a few weeks but I couldn't go with a broken arm. I was so pissed."

Alyssa frowned. "You were crying in bed that night."

Hunt rolled his eyes. "Men don't cry."

"You weren't a man, you were a sad boy. You wanted to go with your father."

He stroked her silky hair. "You came in and gave me your dog, told me he helped you when you missed your daddy." He would never forget that little girl comforting him. Her dad had died, but she was trying to comfort him because he missed out on a trip. Even then, Lyssie was special.

"It made sense to me at the time."

Hunt tugged her head back, looking into her eyes. "And this, holding you and being your friend when you need one, makes sense to me now."

She curled into him, her warmth pushing back years of loneliness, her sunshine and vanilla scent chasing out the stench of death that clung to him.

She stirred in him a longing to be a man capable of love, but that part of him had died out in the deserts of the Middle East. What was left was a man with a switch—when triggered, Hunt went right into sniper mode. A cold hard killer.

• • •

The nightmares woke him. Hunt didn't bother trying to go back to sleep and got up, dragging on a pair of sweats. In the hallway, he paused by the closed door of Lyssie's room. Tonight she'd let him pull her into his lap. But if she knew the things he'd done, she'd never have let him touch her.

Turning away, he headed through the family room, out the sliding glass door, and strode through the gloom of night until he reached the locked studio. He punched in the code to unlock the doors. Once inside, Hunt flipped a switch, and the big space flooded in light, revealing his dark side.

This was what he'd become.

The big shelving unit held dozens of sculptures of war and death. It was the only way he knew to rid himself of the nightmares, and the emotions that broke through his control to boil up in his sleep. For his years as a sniper, he'd disconnected, gone cold. He hadn't looked at his targets as human, but as a job he'd had to do. One that would safeguard hundreds and thousands of lives.

That detachment came home with him and at first he couldn't sculpt at all. Then he'd had the piss-ass luck to be in the mall when a shooter erupted into gunfire. Hunt had been armed and took out the gunman to stop the carnage. Once that was over, his nightmares started. Then all he could sculpt was the death and suffering lining his shelves in the studio.

Shaping, carving and molding his nightmares into three-dimensional clay shapes wrung him out, forcing him to feel every bit of shock, revulsion, regret, fear... All of it that he'd refused to feel at the time he'd done the job. But there was one memory he'd never sculpt, his last mission as a Marine sniper. Hunt had been sent to track another sniper that had completely snapped and started killing. Rand Oliver was highly trained and exceedingly dangerous.

And he'd also once been a friend.

The mission had sucked. Hunt had hoped to get Rand to surrender. Instead, it'd come down to a shootout where only one of them survived.

Chapter Five

Saturday morning, Hunt glanced at the laptop on the kitchen island where Sienna stared back via Skype. "No problems on Griff's end?"

"No. His team has arrived, everything is in place. If anyone is watching the kid, they'll catch them. Do you really think this guy would be dumb enough to go after a kid?"

"He went to the trouble of tracking the kid down and getting photos. I think he's determined to get Lyssie by whatever means it takes." No way would he let that happen.

"Who?"

Huh? Oh. "Alyssa. It's an old nickname. Now that Alyssa and the kid are safe, start an investigation on Nate Madden. Everything you can find on him. From what Alyssa overheard, Madden approached her stepfather with this scheme. Her stepfather isn't the threat." Hunt knew the man vaguely; he'd been the kind of man who tried to own his wife's success. No, Alyssa could handle Parker. It was Nate that caused that tingle on the back of Hunt's neck. "Madden has invested serious time and effort into Alyssa and he's not going away easy."

"On it." Sienna took off her glasses. "I can't believe you knew Alyssa Brooks and never said anything."

"It was a long time ago, Si." He'd thought Lyssie had forgotten him and his family.

"And yet you took her to your home."

"Don't read anything into that."

"Too late. Gotta go." She disconnected.

Hunt shut the laptop and fought a groan. Sienna had lost her husband, Trace, in the line of duty. Now she filled the void by taking care of all of them—her husband's friends. If she got it in her head that he and Lyssie should be together...

Hell no. Hunt wasn't going down that road again. He'd tried, seriously tried, when he returned from the Middle East, absolutely determined to return to civilian life and be normal, but he wasn't and never would be again. All he had to do was recall the mall shooting six weeks after he'd come home. Desperate for normalcy, he began dating Rachel Anderson, who was with him when the mall shooting broke out.

Her horrified voice after it was over rang in his head. *I can't do this. You just killed so easily. One second we were walking along laughing, then the shooting started and you shoved me into a rack of clothes. I didn't even know you had that gun on you. Then you killed that man and didn't even flinch. Like it was nothing.*

Rachel had looked at him like he was an unfeeling monster. When he went into sniper mode, that's exactly what he was. It's what he'd been trained to be and he'd been damn good at it, maybe the best.

He hadn't dated again after that.

Frustration ate at him. Even sculpting hadn't helped last night. The piece, the one that had been haunting his dreams lately, wouldn't come together. Instead, he'd been thinking about Lyssie, the way it felt to hold her, how good she smelled.

Face it, you got the hots for her. Lyssie was off-limits sexually. He'd brought her there to help her, not seduce her. What he needed to do was sculpt for a while. Last night had been an aberration. Once he got his hands on the cool clay, the drive, that wild thumping obsession to give face to his nightmares, bring them into three-dimensional focus and lock them away in his studio, would manifest. His hands tingled with the urge to feel and shape the clay.

Relieved, he headed out the doors into the bright sunlight. Squinting, he scanned over the built-in barbecue with the stone bar surround and stools, the heavy, round wrought iron table, the pool and…Well hell.

Alyssa sat on a lounger. His gaze traveled down her face and slender neck to a strappy white top that left a wedge of her belly bare. A laptop rested on her thighs, and from there her long, bare legs stretched out in sinful temptation.

His blood thumped with a painful shot of pure want, the memory of her scent, the feel of her warm body in his arms. He jerked his attention to the rectangular pool sparkling in the sun. *Get control. Lyssie's not a hookup, and you can't give her more than that.*

The studio. It was right there, maybe forty feet past Lyssie. He'd say a quick hi, then lock himself in the studio, but when he returned his gaze to her, he saw her chewing on a thumbnail. Against his will, his lips curved into a smile.

She'd always done that when she was absorbed or concentrating. What had her so engrossed? Curiosity propelled him into striding over to her. Once there, he couldn't help taking another eye-journey over that top with the crisscrossing straps, then down her belly where his attention caught on a small stylized heart tattoo dipping into her shorts between her belly button and right hip bone. A delicate ruby tear was inked in the center of the tat. His hands twitched with the temptation to touch it.

"You're staring." She tilted her head up from the screen.

He forced his attention to her face. "You have a tattoo."

"Wow, no wonder you're a bodyguard. You don't miss a thing."

He fought a grin. "Careful, smart-mouth girl. The heater's on in the pool." He dragged a chair close to her, dropped onto it and nodded toward her computer. "You were concentrating pretty hard. What are you doing?"

She closed the laptop. "Nothing."

"Liar. You were totally absorbed. Spill it."

"Just playing with some pictures and video. It's not important."

Given the way she had her hand resting on the laptop in a protective gesture, he thought it was very important. "Can I look?"

"There's nothing to see." She tugged the laptop until the edge pressed into her stomach. "It's just a hobby."

"You used to show me your pictures."

She glanced right toward the studio then back to him. "You used to show me your sculptures."

Crap, she had him there. "Stalemate."

She flashed him her real grin, one side of her mouth

tilting up more than the other. "You can always give in and let me see what you're working on at two a.m."

"Were you spying on me?"

"I heard you get up and looked out my bedroom window. I saw the light on in the studio. Do you sculpt a lot at night?"

"Depends."

"On?"

"If I wake up." Time to change the subject. "I just talked to Sienna. She's starting the background check on Nate."

Shoving her laptop aside, she pivoted to face him and dropped her bare feet to the cement. Glancing at her phone by her thigh, she added, "He's been calling for the last hour. I send it to voicemail."

"Have you listened to his message?"

"He says, 'Parker forwarded me your resignation. One chance, Alyssa. Call me before I'm forced to keep my word.'" She twisted her fingers. "He's in Europe, he can't do anything, right?"

Her worry rubbed him like coarse sandpaper. "Not to Eli or you. You're both safe." Hunt would repeat that as many times as it took. "But to keep you both that way, we need to treat Madden as dangerous, and find a way to stop him. That may mean at some point it comes out that you gave birth to Eli."

She lifted her head, shoving up her sunglasses. "I'm not going back and caving in to Nate. I know I've been weak, but this? No. I won't be threatened, bullied, and blackmailed, and I won't let him threaten Eli or his family."

Weak? What he saw was a scared woman who took steps to protect herself and the kid she cared about. No one else had been there to protect her, but now? She had him.

For protection. Not to push her back in that chair and kiss her… Yeah, time to get to work. "Tell me what you know about Madden."

She shifted her gaze to the pool. "He grew up in L.A. Only kid of a single mom, Lorelei Madden. She was a small-time actress, got pregnant and never got another role. I think she ended up becoming a hairdresser."

"Father?"

"Nate didn't know who he was. He grew up without much, and put himself through college and law school. He worked for Clout Law Group until Parker hired him."

"Have you met his mom?"

"She died four years ago."

A prickle zinged down his spine. Madden had told Alyssa in that elevator *I eliminate problems*. Had his mother become a problem? "How did she die?"

"Accident. She fell down the stairs." Her shoulders jacked up as she sucked in a quick breath. "Nate didn't kill her if that's what you're thinking. He didn't even live there, but found her in the morning when he went over." Alyssa scrunched her nose. "She sounded kind of bitter from Nate's description. Thought she should have been this great actress but getting pregnant screwed it up for her. She'd had a couple small roles in forgettable TV shows, and one tiny role in a horror film. She never got her big break. In L.A., that's as common as smog."

"I'll have Sienna contact the police department that was called out to the scene of her accident. Get any reports we can."

She took a deep breath. "It's still hard to believe. A few days ago I was going to marry him, and now we're wondering if he killed his mother."

His muscles tensed at the mention of her belonging to another man. It had been him she'd run to, his arms that held her last night... *Stop it*. In a day's time his old feelings for Alyssa, that big-brother protectiveness, had morphed into something more. Deeper, and much more possessive. Drawn to her in a way that screamed danger, he got up and settled next to her. "You really didn't love Nate."

She lifted her gaze to his. "I wanted a baby and a family. I wanted to be safe and stable in a relationship. I thought about this a lot when I went for a run this morning."

"The one you didn't want me to go on with you?" He'd been making coffee when she came out in a pair of shorts, T-shirt and running shoes.

Shrugging, she answered, "I like to think when I run. I put on my music and go."

Yep, he got that. She was safe on vineyard property as long as she had her cell phone with her. "You ran for over an hour. What did you come up with?"

"Men suck."

Hunt laughed. "Guess you can't get all life's answers in one run. But—"

Lyssie's phone dinged and vibrated by her thigh.

She scooped it up and looked at the screen. "Text from Nate."

"Read it."

Her sun-warmed skin paled. "You're not in your house, but your car is in the garage. Are we going to have a problem I need to eliminate?" Lifting her eyes, worry filled her eyes. "He's threatening me. This is crazy, Nate's in Europe. How does he even know I'm gone but my car is in the garage?"

The back of Hunt's neck prickled with danger. "You're sure he went?"

"Yes. Dragon Wing's limo took him to the airport. I checked with the driver." Alyssa shivered and wrapped her arms around herself. "Someone had to get in my house and garage to realize I'm gone but my car is there."

"Who has a key?"

"Nate, Jessie my housekeeper, and my friend Maxine."

Hunt considered it. He'd seen her gated community in Malibu. "Call the guard shack and see if they have a record of any of them going through the gates."

She picked up her phone, went through her contacts and made the call. Finished, she hung up. "Not Maxine or Jessie, only a dress delivery sent from an up-and-coming designer." She rubbed her forehead. "Those always go to Dragon Wing, never my house. Even if the office sent them there since I quit, they don't have a key and Jessie's not there today." A shudder ran through her. "Someone was in my house. Nate's having me watched."

Lyssie's growing anxiety yanked out his need to protect and soothe her. Care for her. No way in hell would he let her get hurt. He cupped her chin, forcing her to focus on him. "I'll have an operative, Cooper Sims, go to your house in the next few days and sweep it for bugs and cameras. He'll change your locks, and evaluate your security system. By the time he's done, no one will get into your house because it will be a fortress. It's going to be okay."

"Thank you, but I need to pay you too, not just—"

Releasing her chin, he spread his hand over her shoulder, cutting her off. "Don't." He wasn't taking her money. "That bastard scared you. He threatened you and your son. Until

I know you're safe, until I'm one thousand percent sure he won't dare touch you or hurt you in any way, I'm your bodyguard. And you don't pay me for that." The feel of her soft, sun-warmed skin nearly singed his hand, but he stayed on point. "And no one gets through me, Lyssie. No one."

• • •

Alyssa stared into his eyes, soaking up the feel of his hand covering her shoulder. For the first time in years, she felt safe…and more. He sat so close that his scent of soap and male, mixed with clay that always clung to him, teased her. She caught herself inhaling, trying to memorize it. But all it did was fuel her simmering desire. The want she hadn't experienced in years. *Answer him!*

"Okay."

"Good."

He didn't move. He hadn't shaved this morning and the shadow on his jaw added to the edge in him. This wasn't like last night when he'd pulled her into his lap. Oh, there'd been a thrum of sexuality, but mostly it'd been trust and comfort, familiarity. A bond of old friendship.

This? Her pulse jumped, and her nipples tightened from just the touch of his hand. She'd experienced sexual attraction before, but this was insane. It was a raw, penetrating *need*. She licked her lips, trying to think of something clever to say, some way to lighten the moment.

"Don't do that."

His husky growl shivered into her. "What?"

"Lick your lips." He leaned closer, dark intensity throbbing in his voice. "I'm barely holding back."

"From?"

"Kissing you."

Oh God. Alyssa had dreamed of kissing him for years, craved the feel of his arms around her, his mouth exploring hers. Heat curled in her belly and her skin ached for his touch. She couldn't resist, didn't want to, and so leaned closer, desperate to know what Hunt's kiss would be like.

Hunt yanked his hand back, rubbing his palm over his face. "This is not happening."

Everything was changing too fast for her to keep up with. The sudden desire flaring hot and wild between them as if it'd been there for years, but was suddenly released. "I... Wow. I've never felt that before..."

He turned, amusement easing the harsh need that had been stamped on his face. "No?"

"Not that intense." Yeah, she should probably shut up now. Or disappear. Her face heated. "Don't you dare make fun of me. I just haven't had sex in a while, and you're all—" She waved her hand at him in his shorts and T-shirt. "Former Marine, dark and sexy. It happens." *Shut. Up. Please, just stop talking.* She squeezed her eyes shut. "Any chance you could go away and let me drown myself in the pool?"

"Nope." He took her hand. "Eyes on me, cover girl."

Not like she had a choice. He'd sit there all day. She forced her eyes open. "Go ahead, make fun of me."

"I'll make fun of you for a lot of things, but not for telling me the truth about how you feel. Ever. Got it?"

Her humiliation eased. This was the Hunt she'd always known. He'd known she had a crush on him when she'd been a teenager, but he'd been gentle with her feelings then, too. "Maybe I won't drown myself."

One side of his mouth lifted. "I was the one that damn near kissed you. I'd say we're even."

"You really wanted to?"

"Too much. There's something about you that shreds my control and believe me, that's not easy to do. I was wrong to even think about it. You came to me for help, you need space and a friend. Not a man who will use you and walk away."

Alyssa forgot her embarrassment at the hardness settling over him. Her heart twisted. What had happened to him? Was it the friends he'd lost? "Why, Hunt? You said you only have sex, not relationships. Why?"

His mouth tightened and he turned his gaze left.

Alyssa followed, taking in the studio. Once it had been open, full of light and laughter, music playing, with the smell of paint, turpentine and clay. Seeing it closed up tight and locked screamed *wrong* to her. "What do you sculpt that you need to keep locked up?"

He turned back. "What do you take pictures of?"

Did it matter if she told him? The sudden jack in her heart rate and her slick palms said it did—because his opinion mattered. Maybe he'd trust her if she told him. "Real people who overcome and survive. Not carefully crafted Hollywood stories, but real valor that is inspiring. At least to me."

Interest flared in his eyes, shoving back those awful shadows. "More."

Part of her wanted to tell him, but this was her love, her passion, the one thing that was truly hers. Nate and her stepfather had no interest. They were annoyed that she wasted her valuable time on a silly hobby. She had responsibilities, an obligation; after all, her mom had died and left Alyssa wealthy. Wasn't she grateful?

Shutting off the voice in her head, she answered, "No, it's your turn. What do you sculpt?"

"You don't want to know."

Her heart forgot to beat. Alyssa hated the isolation walling him off. He went into his studio at night and what? Last night, when she'd sat on the terrace, cold and alone, he'd pulled her into his arms. Right now she wanted to comfort him. She picked up his hand, cradling it to hers. Alyssa could feel the strength in his fingers, the power in his hand. "Once you sculpted slices of life." Whatever caught his eye, but she'd bet her favorite camera that wasn't what he was sculpting now. "What changed?"

"I was a sniper."

Stunned, she sucked in a breath. "In the Marines?"

He nodded once. "I left when killing became too easy. When the line that separates the good guys from the bad started to blur." Facing her he said, "That wasn't who I wanted to be anymore."

Her chest clenched. What would it take out of a man to do that kind of job? She gripped his hand when he tried to pull away. "Do you regret it?" His dream had been to be a Marine. Had it all turned to a nightmare?

"No. What I did saved countless lives. I'd make the same choice again."

She tried to understand. He'd left because he didn't want to be a sniper anymore. "But you wanted to come home, go back to being who you were... An artist?"

His mouth thinned. "There's no going back. I did the job and live with the consequences. I don't sculpt slices of life anymore." He tugged his hand from hers and stood. "Death.

I sculpt death. And I don't want that to touch you ever."

Oh God. Her heart ached for him as she watched him stride toward the studio, hurting and alone. Unable to bear it, Alyssa jumped up and ran after him. "Hunt, wait!"

He swung around, the sun catching the turmoil riding his eyes and straining the harsh lines of his face. His shoulders jacked beneath his T-shirt. "Stop. Don't touch me."

Freezing one foot away, she tilted her face up. "Why?"

His stare pierced through her, yet he stayed rigidly motionless. "One touch and I'm going to kiss you. Hard. Not like whatever the fuck you were doing with your ex. If I kiss you, you're going to feel my hunger to have you naked, wet, and wild beneath me." He sucked in a hissing breath through his teeth. "I don't want some prissy-ass cover girl, Lyssie, I want you."

This was Hunt uncensored. Not the young adult she remembered, but the damaged, lethal man. She could almost smell his lust, feel his need burning in the spotlight of his eyes. Hot shivers danced in her belly as gooseflesh erupted on her arms. The way he looked at her, seeing her exactly as she was, rolled over her common sense and shattered her reserve. She'd never had this—primitive untamed desire. Desperate to feel more of it, she laid her hand on the warm granite of his arm. "Kiss me. Don't hold back."

Her words hung there for two beats, then Hunt latched his arm around her waist, easily swept her up and spun, pressing her against the side of the art studio. His hard chest pinned hers, his rugged thigh slid between hers, while his gaze raked from her eyes and down to her mouth.

Her lips tingled in response. *From just his look.* She touched her mouth with her fingertips.

Hunt growled, his eyes heating. Gently, he wrapped his fingers around her wrist and tugged, then, with his stare locked on her, he brushed his lips over her fingers and sucked them in.

She couldn't look away. Warm, wet lashes of his tongue bathed each digit. Every stroke arced straight to her nipples and core. She squeezed her thighs around his thick muscular leg. Her breasts swelled and ached, craving the same treatment from his tongue and lips. He hadn't even kissed her yet and she was already on fire. "Hunt."

Easing her fingers out, he laced their hands together and pressed her arm over her head. With his hand on her hip, he dragged her up his thigh.

Dear God. The friction on her clit made her gasp. Hot pleasure swirled in her belly.

Hunt leaned in. "Make that noise again, and I'm going to do more than kiss you."

Nothing had ever been like this. Her entire world narrowed to the two of them. Flames licked at her spine and made her tremble. He hadn't even kissed her, and she nearly wept with need. Shook with it. It took all she had not to rock her hips on this thigh. Somewhere deep in her mind she had an awareness that he was purposely showing her this side of himself, but if he meant to scare her, he'd miscalculated. Because for all the demanding intensity rolling off him, and the sexual heat burning between them, he'd linked his fingers with hers and softly stroked her wrist. She had no fear, just hunger and the need to meet his intensity with her own. "I want to taste you." With her fingers in his hair, she tugged.

• • •

Hunt was screwed. No power on earth could make him deny her. With their hands joined over her head and his other holding her anchored to his thigh, Hunt took her mouth. Lyssie's soft lips parted and he dove in. Her flavor flooded him; he tasted iced tea and lemon, along with that richer flavor that was all Lyssie.

Time ceased to mean anything as he explored her. He slowed his assault, wanting to savor her, to absorb the feel of Lyssie. She tightened her fingers in his hair and stroked her tongue against his. Every soft moan arrowed straight to his cock. It took all his self-control not to lift her higher, spread her legs and rock against her heat. But damn, the taste of this woman drove him to the edge of reason, and the feel of her nipples stiff against his chest, the way her thighs gripped his leg, told him she wanted more.

Oh he'd give her more…

Fuck. What was he doing? *She came to you for help and you're all over her like a rash.* Regret and self-disgust slammed into him. Jerking his mouth back, he eased her to her feet.

Lyssie stared up at him with unfocused and confused eyes, her lips wet and swollen. Her skin was flushed all the way down her slender throat to her white stretch top that outlined her stiff nipples. His hands spasmed at his side. His muscles twitched. Hunt clenched his jaw, squeezed his eyes shut. *Get control, asshole.* Less than a half hour ago, she'd been scared and upset by her ex's text. Hunt brought her home to protect her and give her a place to feel safe. Not seduce her.

His guts churned. He shouldn't have touched Lyssie. She'd told him clearly what she wanted—a family. Not a damaged man like him. She was scared and lost, and had known him since she was a kid. Trusted him.

"I... What happened?"

Snapping his eyes open, he took in her arms crossed in front of her breasts, the warm color draining from her face. Self-consciousness had her pulling in on herself. Furious that he'd done that to her, Hunt said, "I'm the jerk, Lyssie, not you. Get that look off your face." He couldn't stand her doubting herself.

Shame dimmed the fire in her. "I broke up with my fiancé two days ago, and then begged you to kiss me."

Every protective instinct he had went hot. Forgetting his resolve not to touch her, Hunt opened his arms and softened his voice. "Come here."

Without a second's hesitation, she wrapped her arms around him.

That trust nearly undid him and he buried his face in her hair. "I didn't stop because of that asshole. You owe him nothing, not your loyalty or your body, hear me?"

"Damn right."

He smiled at her muffled determination muttered against his chest. That was his girl. "I'm not going to use you for sex. You'll get hurt."

She tilted her head back. "I wanted to kiss you, I just didn't know it'd burn like that."

God, her honesty, he loved that, but he had to end this now or he'd make her burn until she came and then do it again — and again. Then he'd leave her, hurting her and she'd never again trust him enough to walk right into his arms. Hunt needed to be the man she trusted, even for this short time.

"That's why we're not doing it again. That kind of lust gets out of control and you'll end up scorched." *Lying to yourself now?* It wasn't just Lyssie that would get singed. There was something about this woman that was slipping beneath his skin and stirring the embers of a part of him he'd thought long dead. He shoved that away and firmed his voice. "I'm going to be your friend and protector." He carefully set her aside, punched in the code on his art studio, and went inside. Shutting the door, he locked himself in the gloomy darkness and Lyssie out in the bright sunshine.

Where she belonged.

Chapter Six

Around four a.m. Hunt dragged himself into the house. The nightmare had been rough, but trying to expel it into clay and feeling it all had left him empty and tight. His head and muscles ached, and he dropped down on the couch, picking up the remote. Finding a movie, he turned it on low, then settled back. He kicked his bare feet up and willed his body to relax.

He heard her door open. The colorful light from the TV revealed Lyssie shuffling out, wearing a tank and PJ pants, her eyes sleepy, a line creasing her cheek from her pillow. She navigated between the corner sofa and coffee table to stare down at him.

Oh hell no. He couldn't do this now. For three excruciating days and nights, he'd kept his hands off her. "Go back to bed. You don't want to be out here right now."

She tilted her head. "That's not the deal. Only the studio is off-limits." She settled on the couch next to him.

Her warmth flowed over his skin, her scent climbing down his throat. Then she reached out, taking his hand and threading their fingers. Helplessly, he looked down at the smaller hand twined with his. Something in this throat, the tight loneliness that dogged him after sculpting out his nightmares, unlocked. "What are you doing?"

Her brown eyes filled with softness. "Being your friend. Most nights, you go back into your room. Probably watch Netflix on your iPad or read, I don't know, except I know you don't sleep for a while. But tonight, you're out here so I'll keep you company."

The feel of her hand in his warmed his veins, made him want too many things he couldn't have. "You need to sleep." Lyssie had been busy in Skype meetings with her accountants and lawyers. Controlling her wealth was complex, plus she still owned half of Dragon Wing, and then she ran several charities with her assistant Maxine. On top of that she had her secret project…something to do with her pictures. All this and the stress that asshole Madden's threats put on her were exhausting. He was tempted to pick her up and dump her in her bed—but he'd never walk out.

"I can multitask." Gripping his hand in both of hers, she curled up next to him, laying her head against his shoulder. "Unless you really want to be alone?"

He should. Jesus, he should send her back to her room. Did she know what a temptation she was to him with her full mouth, sleepy eyes and too-generous heart? How god-damned sexy she looked, or the way her hair sliding over his arm sent wake-up messages to his cock?

It'd be so much easier if their attraction was only physical. That he knew how to deal with. He'd give them both what they wanted until they were satisfied. But this? Fuck. Lyssie had come to him, turned to him when she'd been scared and desperate. That's who he wanted to be. Sex would destroy that and them, because eventually, she'd learn who and what he really was. Then she'd look at him with horror and turn away.

"Hunt?"

Do it. Tell her to go back to bed. Or get up and walk away from her. But he wasn't that strong. Instead, he pulled her into his arms, settling her against his chest. He grabbed the blanket off the back of the couch and covered her. "Stay."

An hour later, Hunt laid her in her bed. Lyssie was sound asleep and so damned beautiful, she took his breath away. Every cell in his body cried out to slide into that bed with her, kiss her awake. His heart pounded and stomach muscles contracted sharply. Need clawed him.

But he walked out and quietly closed her door.

• • •

"Hey, there you are."

Alyssa jerked, almost falling off the barstool.

Hunt caught her arm. "Whoa, didn't mean to scare you."

"Dang." Slapping a hand against her chest, she sucked in air. He was fresh from his shower after his morning run and workout. They both loved running, but she kept to her isolated runs, and Hunt never pushed to join her.

This morning, she'd run twice her normal miles, trying to beat her growing desire into submission, the ache that woke her in the nights and stole her thoughts in the day. Hunt set the ground rules: friends only. She had to respect that, but then she'd come out here early this morning and found him sitting on the couch, so alone her heart cracked. She'd needed to touch him, and he'd let her by pulling her into his arms, wrapping the throw blanket around her and stroking her hair. She'd fallen asleep like that, with his heart beating against her skin.

Now she was awake. Every nerve ending lighting up, her mouth drying as Hunt's soap and clay scent filled her lungs. The memory of his arms around her ignited her longing, her lips tingled with the echoes of that kiss four days ago. In less than a week with Hunt, she felt more alive and real than she had in the last seven years.

Say something! She lifted her gaze to his blue eyes and her chest pinged like she was fourteen years old again. He hadn't let go of her upper arm, just loosened his hold, and rubbed his thumb over her skin. Tingles spread from that tiny touch. "Why were you looking for me?"

He finally released her arm and leaned against the counter. "I have some updates."

Anxiety chased out her desire. "What?"

Hunt's eyes flattened. "Cooper Sims said your house is clean of bugs and cameras and he even had a mechanic go over your car. He's changed all the locks and upgraded your security system."

Wow, that was thorough. "So you don't think anyone was in my house?"

Hunt's jaw bulged. "Depends. What did you do with your engagement ring when you broke up with Madden?"

"Gave it back." She mentally retraced her steps. "I set it on the desk outside Nate's office. He saw me. Why?"

Hunt pulled out his phone and held it up.

As soon as she saw the picture, shock twanged in her head. Her huge single-cut diamond ring in the platinum setting sat on a black cloth spread on her gold bedspread. "He had someone get into my house and leave the ring on my bed."

Hunt rubbed her arm. "That's a stalker move, Lyssie. He's showing you he can get into your bedroom anytime he wants, even when he's out of the country. It's not Parker doing it for him. We're having him watched. Besides, the guards at the entrance would recognize him."

"Probably." She looked up. "Nate's having me watched, isn't he?"

"I believe so, and for a long time." He put his phone away. "Nate appeared obsessed with you when he worked at Clout Law Group."

She tried to process it. "I hadn't even met him then. Parker introduced Nate to me after he hired him." It felt like she was spinning in a whirlpool.

"You're a powerful woman who's on TV all the time. Cooper, Sienna, and I think he targeted you and worked through Parker to get to you. That he's been watching you for a while, and had people inside Dragon Wing that were gathering information for him. That's how he figured out how to approach and win you over." He took a breath. "Do you trust your assistant, Maxine?"

"Yes. 100 percent."

Leaning an arm on the counter, he studied her. "Why?"

"I fired two assistants, Noreen Atkins for taking pictures of me and posting them on social media, and then Shea Foley for going through my things. That's when I offered Maxine the job. She and Nate hate each other. Seriously hate each other."

"Could be an act."

"Maxine befriended me in college. She's the one who forced me to start driving again."

Surprise flashed over his face. "You stopped driving?"

"After the accident I was scared, terrified. I relied on drivers, but Maxine was having none of that and made me do it. She pushed me to be independent. She knows who I am, but she's never asked me for anything. She's my friend." Alyssa held up a hand. "Before you ask, I never told her about Eli. I met her after I gave him up."

"Okay." Hunt met her stare. "There's more."

Her heart ballooned in her chest at the seriousness of his tone. "What happened?"

"About four a.m. this morning, Griff caught a guy tampering with Eli's family SUV in the driveway. Griff detained him, the police were called." Hunt reached for her hand. "The brake lines were cut."

The horror of it gripped her throat as memories of the car sliding out of control, spinning wildly, slamming into the tree and the crunching metal all came back to her.

"Lyssie." Hunt wrapped his hands around hers. "Look at me."

His command gave her a focus, a way out of her memories. His face, cut harder from years of living a life she couldn't even fathom, eased her sick fear. "Nate did it. He somehow did this."

"Did he know you didn't drive for a while after the accident?"

She nodded. Alyssa had told Nate, tried to make him understand how good a friend Maxine was to her. "He would hurt them. Eli and his family have done nothing to him, yet he'd hurt them. What kind of monster does something like that?" And she'd been engaged to him. "Wait, Griff caught the guy?"

"Yes. Police came, he was arrested, but it's going to take time to see if we can connect him to Madden, although I doubt it's going to be easy. Madden clearly isn't stupid, so I'm sure he's covered his tracks." He squeezed her fingers. "The good news is Madden will know that we have Eli protected and he can't get to him. Griff has an entire team watching the family, including while they sleep."

She had to know. "Was Eli scared?"

"He never woke up and doesn't know what happened. His parents have told him the guys are following the family around for a special work project his father is working on. According to Griff, Eli accepts that and thinks it's cool."

A painful mix of relief, happiness, and pain so deep it scared her, twisted in her chest. Everything in her wished she could have been strong enough to be the parent Eli had needed, but she hadn't been, not then. The old grief, the pain she'd refused to let out rose up to choke her. She had the urge to throw herself into Hunt's arms now, and beg him to hold her. But then she'd break. Not happening. Instead she slipped her hands from his and pulled herself together. "So what do we do now?"

He eyed her. "Are you okay?"

"Pissed. Furious. But I'll be fine." She would be, she just had to pull herself together. Shutting her laptop, she grabbed her coffee cup and headed around the island to the coffeemaker. There she stared at the carafe. "What do we do next?"

"Let us investigate. Sienna's requested the reports on Madden's mom's death. She should have those soon. We'll work to find out who hired the guy arrested this morning."

Alyssa nodded, staring at the coffeemaker.

"But right now—"

She jumped, the coffee cup clanking on the countertop. He was right behind her. So close, his breath stirred her hair. How did he move so quietly?

Reaching around her, he shut off the coffeemaker.

His arm brushed hers, his chest pressing against her back. Solid warmth. She desperately wanted to lean back against him.

"—we need a break."

She recoiled slightly. Looking over her shoulder, she asked, "From each other?"

"From the stress. We've been cooped up here for days. Let's go have some fun. So far, no one knows you're here, so it should be safe as long as you do as I say."

"Really?" Excitement chased out the thick worry and dread. "Where?"

"It's a surprise." Turning her to face him, he glanced down at her dress, his eyes regretful. "You'll have to put on more clothes. Jeans and either athletic shoes or boots. I have a jacket and helmet you can use. Bring your camera too."

Anticipation buzzed her veins. "You still have your motorcycle?" She used to beg him to take her on his motorcycle. Her mother had said no, though, so Hunt refused, although she'd taken a million pictures of him on it.

Humor glinted in his light eyes. "I have a different bike than you remember, this one is faster." He flashed her a grin, stripping away the years that had passed between them. She wasn't the infamous Alyssa Brooks trying to fill her dead mother's shoes, and Hunt wasn't a Marine veteran carrying internal wounds he vented in his art. They were Hunt and Lyssie, ready to ride.

• • •

Hunt loved the speed and freedom of riding, the sensation of going fast enough to outrun the consequences of his choices.

Total illusion. He couldn't outrun a bullet, not even on a bike this fast. He knew exactly how to calculate the speed of the bike against the distance between him and his target to make the shot. But right now, with Lyssie pressed against his back, her thighs around his hips, and the wind in their faces, he felt boundless as if anything were possible again. Even with her as just a friend felt pretty damn good. He'd known suggesting a bike ride would wipe that tight tension off her face and make her smile. Much better than when she'd pulled her hands from his when she'd been upset.

He wanted her to walk into his arms, not pull away.

After an hour of riding, he slowed near the shack surrounded by other bikes and a few cars. This place was way off the beaten path, mostly known to locals. He doubted anyone would recognize Lyssie. She had her hair tightly braided, no makeup on, and wore one of his leather jackets. She looked like his Lyssie, not the glamorous Alyssa Brooks. Since no one knew she was here, she should be safe. He was armed and prepared just in case.

As he stopped the bike and killed the engine, the scent of tacos filled the air. "Still up for doing this?" Rough wood picnic tables spread out along the sloping dirt at the side of the taco stand.

"Yes, is this like a biker hangout?" Holding on to his shoulders, she swung her long leg off the bike and peered down at him.

He missed her against his back and her arms wrapped around him the second she was gone. Putting the bike on the kickstand, he got off, removed his helmet and retrieved her camera bag, throwing the strap over his shoulder. "Locals who know about it, mostly bikers and a few hikers. Some tourists find it too."

She studied the flat-roofed shack with the large ordering window below the handwritten menu. A scraggly line of about seven bearded men and one woman all wearing biker gear waited their turn. Out at the tables, a few more attacked their food. "It's remote. I mean, I hear the ocean hitting the rocks, but can't see the shoreline from here. This isn't where you open a taco stand to get rich."

He placed their helmets on the bike, then reached for her hand and led her to the line. He couldn't see her eyes behind her sunglasses, but her face was flooded with color. So damn pretty. He wanted to put that pink glow on her skin with his kiss and—

Nope, not going there. Instead he focused on her question. "The owner is a veteran, lost his leg to a roadside bomb. Lost a lot of friends that day too. He doesn't want to be in the middle of town. Here there's only one road in and out and that gives him a sense of control."

She angled her face toward the shack, her lines screaming compassion. "How long have you known him?"

"Years. Found this place when I was home on leave." Hunt had become more and more solitary, taking long motorcycle rides.

"And most of these guys, they're vets too?"

Her words pulled him back to the beautiful woman wearing his jacket. It was too big for her but she didn't seem to care. She was more interested in the people around them than herself. "Most, yeah."

"Do you know them all?"

He shrugged. "No, but they won't bother you. These guys want their space. Stay out of their way, and you'll be fine." They were quickly moving up the line. "What do you want to eat?"

"Two carne asada tacos and extra guacamole. Iced tea."

Hunt turned to place their orders, paid, and handed Lyssie her box of tacos and chips with extra guacamole. They found a picnic table and dug in.

"I didn't think to bring cash with us. Sorry. I'll pay you back at the house."

Hunt set down his drink and taco and shoved up his shades. "For two tacos and a drink?"

"Plus yours." She threw it off, not really paying attention. "These are so good." Closing her mouth around another bite, her eyelids drifted shut and she let out a tiny sound.

A moan.

Damn. That was hot, but wait, she was distracting him. "That what you usually do?"

She grabbed a paper napkin and wiped her lips. "Eat like this? No, but man I have to find tacos like this back home."

"Alyssa."

She stopped halfway into another bite.

He could feel her eyes on his, questioning. "Do you pay for everyone else around you?" Like that bastard she'd been engaged to?

Her eyebrows drew together over her sunglasses. "Nate liked flashing the company credit card, so not really. Although I usually reimbursed the company if our meals were private, but..." She shook her head, clearing some memory. "Anyway, this is different."

"Damn right. You are one of mine and you don't pay me back for a couple tacos."

Her tongue darted out as she licked her lips then said, "One of your what?"

Hunt finished off his first taco, and eyed her. "Friends. The kind I drop everything to protect." That clear enough for her?

Her face broke into a huge smile. "Hmm, so who else is on this list?"

Hunt rolled his eyes yet his guts twanged at her very real grin. "Well, my boss Adam has a couple dogs. They are both on the list. But you're right below them."

"Ha ha. I'm not sure you're on any of my lists."

The mood from earlier in his kitchen had lightened, and he was glad to see her having fun. "I'm on your Hot Guy Crush list."

"You just fell below the dude who made these tacos." She picked up her second one and bit into it. "Oh yeah."

His blood heated and raced south. When the hell had watching a woman eat messy tacos become sexy? She had a tiny spot on her lip and he itched to lick it off.

She glanced around. "You know what I like?"

"Me. We've established that. And FYI, I can kick taco guy's ass so he drops below me on your Hot Guy Crush list." He was only half joking. The idea of her crushing on any other man annoyed him.

Alyssa laughed. "Until you make tacos like this? You're second. He's first."

"Nope, I'm first. I brought you here. You'd never have known about these tacos if I hadn't shown you." He leaned forward. "You're the only person I've ever brought here. Put me back at number one." He heard himself, felt the dumbass grin tugging his mouth. She brought out a side of him he hadn't seen in years.

"That's a coveted position, Marine. You want it, you're going to have to earn your way in."

This woman had been featured in magazines as one of the most beautiful executives, but those pictures didn't hold a candle to her now. The wind and helmet had teased pieces of hair from her braid, her skin was slightly wind burned, his black leather jacket had bulked her up, and she was gorgeous. "I'm first, cover girl. We both know it." He pushed his empty box away and wiped his hands. "Now tell me what you like?"

After taking a drink of her tea, she said, "I like that no one's here to be seen. No one cares what everyone else looks like. They really do leave us alone." She shoved up her sunglasses, her eyes connecting with his. "Is that why you haven't shown anyone else this place? You like the solitude?"

Ah, she had been listening. "Come on, I'll show you. This is where you can take some pictures."

• • •

Alyssa took his hand and followed Hunt along a rocky, steep trail leading down. The scent of the ocean, foliage, and damp earth surrounded them. When they stopped at the edge of a cliff overlooking the ocean, Alyssa caught her breath. Jagged rocks led down to foamy water. In one spot, rocks stretched out into the ocean like a finger. "It's breathtaking. Untamed and yet peaceful."

Hunt held out her camera. "Go ahead, you know you want to."

Oh, she did. She stripped off her jacket, laid it on a nearby boulder and took the camera. Quiet flowed through her as she raised her camera and began taking shots. This place felt alive and powerful, a true representation of Mother Nature. Finished with that, she turned and began snapping pictures of Hunt. He'd taken off his jacket too, leaving him in faded jeans and a T-shirt stretched across a wall of muscle. With his legs braced apart, arms crossed, and his eyes constantly moving and scanning, he gave off a sense of a predator ready to spring at any second. But when his gaze slid to her, his mouth softened in a familiar half smile that woke up her entire body.

You're the only person I've ever brought here.

He'd shared this with her, only her. Alyssa's heart clenched as she realized how big a step that must be for Hunt. And that wasn't all—he'd shared what he sculpted in that locked room—death. He didn't want that to touch her, but he'd brought her here, to another private part of his life.

Before she could chicken out, she switched to her stored photos in her camera and pulled up one of her favorites. She blurted out, "Do you still want to see what I take pictures of?"

Hunt dropped his arms and closed the distance between them. "Very much."

What would he think? Her shoulders tensed until her neck ached. "It's just pictures."

He shifted his weight, leaning into her. "That you care about."

Sucking in a breath, she nodded. "This one is of Treva and her service dog. This girl is special. At fifteen, she was hit by a car while riding her bike, and the accident left her a paraplegic. I met her through the canine companion program. Her dog, Sabrina, goes with her everywhere, including college. They have this amazing bond."

"Show me."

She swallowed against the sudden dryness in her throat and tilted her camera so he could see the viewing screen. Treva was bent over in her wheelchair and the dog was stretching up, pressing her muzzle against the girl's cheek. In it, Alyssa saw an authentic and touching moment of affection that transcended species. But would Hunt see it? She rocked on her feet and bit her lip. Every second that he studied the picture felt like an hour.

Finally he shifted his eyes to hers. "Capturing that friendship is art."

That made her want to share more. She flipped through her pictures and found the one she wanted. It was a twenty-something man in a hospital bed, his tattooed arm stretched to clasp hands with an older man in another hospital bed. The caption read: *Son gives father kidney to save his life.*

"How did you get this?"

"The son is a sound engineer for Dragon Wing and I heard about him donating a kidney to his dad, so I asked him if I could take a few photos."

"It's moving and beautiful."

Her throat tightened while her chest swelled. "Thank you." The intensity of his gaze caused her nerves to tingle with the urge to lean into him. "And for bringing me here. The bike ride, the tacos, this view, it's perfect." They stood so close, the heat and bulge of his biceps brushed her shoulder. Alyssa sucked in her breath. "Uh, I should put this away."

"I should let you. Walk away, Lyssie."

His voice dropped to a sexy growl, freezing her in place while his eyes churned like the sea below them. The wind swept over the cliffs, whipping his hair around his harsh face. "Do you know how damned hard it was to put you in bed this morning and walk away?" He laid his hand on her face and dragged his thumb over her lips. "I wanted to kiss you until you woke, slow and soft, your body heating as I tasted you. You'd have let me do that, wouldn't you?"

"Yes." Did her answer get lost in the roar of the waves and the pounding of her heart? The heat of his stare and the way he stroked her lips unleashed spirals of heat in her belly. Her nipples tightened beneath her shirt.

"I wouldn't have stopped there. I'd have peeled off your top, then your pants, until you were bare for me."

She squeezed her thighs together, her skin aching at his words and the sensual images.

"Unless you told me to stop."

Her eyes snapped to his. "I wouldn't have." Right now, out here in the small clearing on the cliffs secluded by rocks and trees, she blurted out the truth. "For years, I've done what everyone else wants me to do. Been what they wanted." Wrapping her hand around his, she pressed his palm to her cheek. "But you, Hunt, you're what I want."

Hunt pulled the camera off her neck, set it in her bag,

then fisted her braid in his hand, lowering his mouth to hers. Her stomach flipped as his taste triggered a wild hunger. Opening beneath him, she slid her tongue against his while her hands roamed over his T-shirt, desperate to learn the shape of him. To feel the years of experience and training that had taken the boy into this man.

Wrapping his arm around her waist, he lifted her, sat on a boulder and pulled her down to straddle him. Tugging her head back, he trailed his hot, damp mouth over her jaw to the delicate spot on her throat.

Oh God. Streaks of heat and pleasure raced to her nipples. Hot chills chased over her nerves, and she pressed down on his hips while digging her fingers into his thick, silky hair. A moan rolled out of her mouth when he rocked his erection through her leggings and panties. The ache there opened wide, desperate. Biting her lip, she tried to pull Hunt to her mouth.

His lips closed over her nipple shielded only by the thin fabric of her T-shirt. "Oh." She arched her back and the hot wet sensation went straight to her clit. When he switched to the other nipple all thoughts melted. It'd never been like this, as if her body recognized this man and melted for him. She tugged on his hair.

Raising his head, his eyes collided with hers. "Lyssie." Her name erupted from him in a gravelly tone. Cupping his other hand around her head, he pulled her in for another kiss. His mouth fused to hers, filling the starving places in her as he stroked her belly beneath her shirt, sliding his fingers over her tender skin up to her nipples and down. "I can't stop touching you. Kissing you."

"Don't stop." Hunt's touch, his hands and mouth, felt

too good. Her belly coiled and tightened. Need clamped hard. She jerked her head back, gasping. "Hunt, oh God. It's been too long, I'm too close."

His gorgeous eyes flared into light and dark, hot and cold, need and emotion. "I love when you do that." All the while, he stroked up and down her stomach, his fingers capturing a nipple then down. The hottest thing was the way he looked at her, his eyes consuming hers.

"What?"

"When you tell me exactly what you're feeling. What you need." He leaned closer. "You can say stop anytime." He slid his fingers beneath her pants but over her panties, circling her clit. "Jesus, you're wet, swollen. So fucking hot."

She dug her fingers into the slab of his shoulders, but it was his eyes that kept her pinned as he slid his fingers beneath her panties, stroking her clit, faster, harder, until all she knew was hot pleasure twisting tighter and Hunt's gaze darkening with heat. "That's it, baby girl. So goddamned sexy."

A bolt of white-hot pleasure streaked down. Her muscles froze. Her breath locked. A second later, the tension exploded in an orgasm. Sounds spilled from her mouth while her body spun out in a wave of pulsing sensation.

Chapter Seven

He'd never seen or felt anything as breathtaking as Lyssie coming apart from his touch. This moment filled an emptiness inside of him. She had trusted him fully, completely. Drawing in a breath and savoring the feel of a warm satisfied woman in his arms, he felt a flicker of hope. Was he changing? Finally getting control of the trained killer inside him?

His cock throbbed with vicious need, but he'd wait. She'd already given him more than he deserved. Instead, he lifted her off her knees and across his thighs to cradle her against him. Hunt rubbed her back, easing her down from a sexual high he didn't think she'd experienced before. Shudders ran through her, but her muscles relaxed. However, she had her head buried in his neck.

Tugging her braid, he looked into her eyes. "You okay?"

Color stained her face. "It's never been like that. I didn't..." She trailed off and she turned her face away. "It's been a long time, I guess."

"You better not be apologizing."

That got her attention and that flicker of shame lost out to a smile that punched him in the chest. Her eyes glowed with golden lights. "It was pretty amazing. I wasn't thinking about anything but how good it felt to be kissed and touched by you. You totally ruined boring sex for me."

Hell, he didn't want to think of her having sex with anyone but him. Possessiveness drove him to take her mouth again, driving his tongue into her sweet heat. But it wasn't enough.

It'd never be enough. The kiss fired his lust into full-bore flames. He tugged his mouth away, dragging in air.

"Are we stopping?"

Her brown eyes shimmered. Strands of her hair had escaped the braid to whip around her face. Her mouth was pink and swollen from his kiss. She took his breath away and destroyed his self-control. There was no resisting her, not if this was what she really wanted.

"Only long enough for me to get you home. Then if you want this, we're going to finish this with both of us coming. Hard and wild." He was losing his mind and too damn close to fucking her right here out in the—

A flash. It came from that cluster of trees ahead and to his left.

Instinct kicked in. His blood iced. Lust forgotten, Hunt lifted Lyssie up, twisted and shoved her over the boulder. "Get down." Yanking his gun from the ankle holster, he leaped up. Had it been the sun glinting off the metal of a weapon? Adrenaline powered through him as he trained his gun to the area the flash came from.

Lyssie grabbed his arm. "What's going on?"

"Down!" He snapped the command while scanning, straining to see, hear or feel any sign of trouble. "I saw a flash."

She crouched behind the boulder. "From what? A camera?"

Hunt swallowed the instinct to order her to be silent. If it was a gun, they already had Lyssie and him in their sight. "Sun glinting off something. Let's go." The switch had been flipped and he was in 100 percent protect or kill mode. Keeping his body between Lyssie and the area it came from, he took her arm, quickly helped her climb over the boulder and headed to his bike. Someone had gotten into Lyssie's house. Had they found her here in Sonoma?

The other men they passed took in the gun he held and the hardness on his face and scattered. He ushered Lyssie on his bike and headed home.

Once back at the vineyard, Hunt set the alarm, then strode into the office that overlooked the front terrace and slapped his hands down on the desk. Anxiety burned up his spine, the adrenaline keeping him wired, edgy.

That flash... Shit. What had it been? Turning, he saw Lyssie in the doorway gnawing on her lower lip. He needed to work through every possibility. "Have you had death threats? Aside from Nate's threat?"

She wrapped her arms around herself and leaned back against the doorjamb. "Not since my mom died. Police handled those."

Shit, that distracted him for a minute. "What kind of death threats?"

"Some of my mom's fans—you know the type. They were angry, believing I killed her. But nothing came of it. It was just a few unhappy people venting about the spoiled, worthless heiress. Most were more a social commentary than threat. The world would be a better place if I died instead of my mom kind of thinking."

She'd been seventeen, damn it. What was wrong with people, saying shit like that? Never mind, that was seven years ago and he needed to focus on the present. Lyssie attracted worldwide attention. "Nothing since then?"

"No. Who would know I'm here?"

"There's always a way." They'd already checked her phone for any tracking devices and turned off her GPS. And Hunt made sure they weren't followed. But they weren't hiding her as much as keeping her safe, so it was possible she'd been found.

"Do you really think it could have been a gun?"

Her question hammered him. For a few minutes out there today, he'd begun to wonder, to hope, that maybe he was changing, becoming more man than killer. For the last few days, there'd been moments in his studio when his need to sculpt nightmares and death had softened into a desire so sculpt beauty. To sculpt Lyssie. Out there on the cliffs, he'd had that fragile hope that she was bringing him back, resurrecting the man he'd once been. Then he'd seen that flash and the switch had flipped. Now she stood there, chewing her lip, hunched in on herself.

"We can't discount any possibility." Tiredness crept in as the adrenaline drained. He dragged his gaze over her. *Shit.* "Your hand." He strode to her, grabbed it up, turning her palm over to the angry red scratches and scrapes. "I hurt you." Dropping her hand as if burned, he backed up to the desk.

"It's a scrape, not even bleeding." She pushed off the doorjamb, slipped out of his jacket, and approached him.

"What happened out there? It was so quick, we were kissing and you were telling me you wanted me then *boom* you were suddenly ready to kill."

He stared down at her. It was the truth and there was no sugarcoating it. "I was ready to kill. It's what I'm trained to do." More. Make her understand. "It's what I am, Lyssie. A killer."

. . .

Shock vibrated through her body. She knew he'd been a sniper, that he'd said killing got to be too easy, but... "No. You're a man who did a job." A hard one that had obviously marked him. "But you're home now."

"You don't get it. The only way I could do my job was to learn to shut down. It became automatic, a switch. Now that I'm home, I still have the same switch. Today, when I saw that flash, the switch flipped and I was a sniper. So heartless that I threw you over a goddamned rock."

Alyssa flinched at the rage in his voice. Unable to bear it, she stroked the bulge in his jaw. "You didn't throw me. It was more of a gentle shove. You think you're the first bodyguard to physically move me when they saw danger?"

"You're not afraid of me?"

"I could never be afraid of you."

Regret etched onto his face. "You say that now until something worse happens and you see what I really am."

"What do you mean?"

Hunt got up and went to the floor-to-ceiling window. With his back to her, he said, "I really thought I could leave it all behind, come home and be normal. I began dating

Rachel, a kindergarten teacher."

He didn't look at her, but stared out to his memories. *Memories of another woman.* Alyssa shook that off; she didn't have any right to be jealous. "What happened?" Did he love her and lose her somehow?

His shoulders tensed, bulging beneath his T-shirt. "We were dating a few weeks when we stopped at the mall on our way to dinner. She wanted to pick up a gift for her father."

Going to him, she reached out to put her hand on his back. His muscles contracted, but she kept her hand in place, just letting him know she was there.

He sighed. "A man stormed into the store with an automatic rifle and started shooting. That was it, the switch in me flipped. I shoved Rachel into a clothing rack and went into full sniper mode. The police weren't there yet and it was a bloodbath. Pulling my gun, I circled around him, lined up a shot and took him out."

Her mind spun, thoughts tumbling so fast she dug her fingers into him to find her balance. "I heard about that shooting." Witnesses talked about the man who killed the gunman, called him a hero. That was Hunt? Just home from the war and walked into that? "But I never heard you were connected with it."

He shifted his eyes to hers. "My name wasn't released. I was cleared, there were plenty of witnesses and I had a license to carry my gun. The case was closed and the media had bigger stories to move on to."

"God, that must have been awful. Here you just left a battlefield… Wait. What about Rachel? Was she hurt?" Her pulse jacked up. Had his girlfriend been shot? Had he lost her?

"She needed a couple stitches in her head from where I'd thrown her into the clothes rack." After a weighty pause, he added, "When I tried to help her stop the bleeding, she freaked and screamed at me not to touch her. She saw me kill the gunman and was horrified." Hunt's temple bulged, tendons stood out on his neck. "She tried to crawl away from me."

"Oh, Hunt, it was just shock." Right?

He shook his head. "That's what I thought too, but a week later, we met up for coffee and she told me she couldn't be with someone like me."

"I'm sorry." Her chest ached for him. "Did you love her?"

"No. She was so normal, a kindergarten teacher." He stared out into the bright sunlight. "I thought I could be normal too, but that day proved I'll never be normal." He fisted his hands on the casing of the window. "She was scared of me."

The pain in those last words burned her heart. Ducking beneath his arm, she wrapped her arms around his waist. "You saved her life and a lot of other lives. She should have been grateful, not scared." Whoever this Rachel was, Alyssa didn't like her.

"Lyssie, she needed stitches. I shoved her in pure instinct, just like I tossed you over the boulder."

She pressed her face against his chest. "You didn't toss me, you *urged* me over." With a tiny bit of force. "I'm sorry she got hurt, but that reaction is unfair."

"It was honest. She told me the truth and believe it or not, I appreciate that. Rachel's a nice girl—"

She tensed with a pang of unfamiliar jealousy.

"—and she told me before I cared too much. Letting her go was easy enough, but I won't forget that fear in her. I won't put another woman through that. You saw how easy it was for my switch to flip today."

"Hunt—"

He tugged her head back. "I shouldn't have kissed and touched you out there today. I took you on a ride because I wanted to share the tacos and the cliffs with you, not seduce you. I don't deserve to touch you like that."

"You do." She reached up to run her fingers on the hard cut of his jaw. "I asked you to kiss me, I begged you to keep going." She hated that he was pulling back from her. He'd given her so much, she wanted to give him whatever he needed—comfort or sex or both.

His eyes burned. "If you ask me again, I won't stop until we're both so satisfied we can't walk, but not today." The harsh lines on his face softened. "I can see it in your eyes that you want to comfort me like you did when you were a little girl and you came into my room to give me your stuffed dog, but you can't. Stuffed animals, sex or love can't fix this. I made choices that changed me forever and I won't subject a woman or children to that." He tugged her hand off his face and held it for a second. "I don't want to hurt you. Make sure you understand that what we can have is a few days or weeks of sex together, but it's not a relationship. Or we can stay friends like we are now." He dropped her hand and walked out.

She hadn't been able to save her mom. Hadn't been able to keep her son. Why would she ever think she could help Hunt?

• • •

"Okay, spill it. What's on your mind?"

Sitting out on the terrace, Alyssa shifted her gaze from the view of the vineyards down to Maxine on the computer's Skype program. They'd begun canceling wedding plans, which would set off a firestorm. That's why Alyssa waited until Friday afternoon when the news cycle slowed.

Wishful thinking.

She shook that off. She didn't owe the world an explanation about her private life. Refocusing on Maxine, she said, "What do you mean? We've gotten a ton done here."

Maxine lifted her chin so that her perfectly straightened blonde hair brushed her shoulders. "No, I've gotten a ton done while you stared off into space, dreaming of your bodyguard."

"Hush." She looked around, concerned Hunt could be standing behind her. The man moved like a ghost when he wanted to. "We're friends." He'd told her to take some time, think about what she wanted, and understand that they didn't have a future together if they crossed the line from friends to lovers.

"Friends that kiss you into an orgasm."

Maxine had pulled that little detail out of her. "It's too soon, right? Even if it's a fling, I just broke up with Nate and—"

"Stop it, Alyssa." Her assistant's face softened. "I don't know Hunt, so maybe it's a fling for him, but not you, and that's what has you scared. You have real feelings for him. Before now, they were a fantasy, a dream, and safe. Now it's real, and you feel for him unlike you've felt for anyone else in your life."

Maxine knew her too well. "But—"

"Not done. So yeah, you might sleep with him, fall hard and end up hurting if it has to end. What you have to ask yourself is which would be worse? To take this time with Hunt and have the memories even if you get hurt? Or chicken out and always wonder?"

Dang. She had a point. The accident that killed her mom had taught her that life could be cut short. She didn't know how many chances at something special she would have.

"Changing the subject, any more leads on who got into your house?"

Anxiety twisted her stomach. Maxine didn't know that Eli existed or that he'd been threatened, or that their family car had been tampered with. "No. They had a key and the alarm code. Nate gave it to them." Alyssa didn't know how this was going to end. "I don't know what's going to happen when Nate gets back this weekend."

"Doesn't matter because you're staying there with Hunt. Shark-Nate-O is dangerous."

Hot suspicion pulsed in her veins. "Has he threatened you?"

Maxine pulled her mouth tight. "He's made a lot of threats, including one that he was going to tell you I came onto him if I didn't quit. He wanted me gone. I had too much influence over you."

It was true. Nate hated Maxine and tried a few times to find ways to get rid of her. "What happened?"

"I laughed in his face and told him to do it. Then you'd know what a lying piece of shit he was."

"Why didn't you tell me?"

She shook her head. "Nate would have spun it, told you it was a joke or something. You were figuring out that he's an ass on your own. I could see it, especially in the last two months. You had enough people pushing you around, but no one is as awesome a friend as me."

That made her smile. "And modest."

Maxine waved that off. "Nate thinks he owns you. It's freaking weird, and Parker just goes along with him. This is going to get ugly when Nate realizes he's lost control of you. Stay away from here. You're safer there with Hunt."

Fifteen minutes later, she closed her computer and headed inside to put it away. Noise in the kitchen stopped her. Hunt was browning meat on the stove. "Oh, I didn't know you were in here." She'd thought he'd probably be out in his studio.

He glanced back over his shoulder. "Starting spaghetti for dinner."

Hugging her computer, his words from two days ago flooded her brain. *If you ask me again, I won't stop.* She wanted that with him, wanted it all since they'd made out on the cliffs two days ago. She wanted to see, feel, and experience him losing control like she had. Did he think about it? Or was it just her? "Do you think about it?" It came out before she could censor her words. That was another thing he did to her—with Hunt she could be honest and real.

He adjusted the heat on the stove, pivoted and moved up to her. "Think about what?"

He was so close she could feel the heat of his skin. "The cliffs. Finishing what we started." It came out as a whisper.

Heat leaped into his eyes and he leaned closer. "The

feel of you coming on my hand, the taste of your mouth and those moans you made live in my memory, keeping me hard and hungry for you. But I won't push you for sex. You will only come to me if that's what you want. What you need." Tension snapped between them. "No one is going to use you again, baby girl."

Her stomach flipped, then fluttered. How did he affect her so deeply? Make her want with a longing that she'd never experienced before?

He eased back a step. "Go put your computer away and get ready for dinner."

Indecision held her to the floor for several heartbeats, but finally she did as he asked. Hunt wasn't going anywhere and they could talk during dinner. Going into her room, her heart froze. There on the dresser was a sculpture. Hunt must have put it there. Her pulse zigzagged in a wild beat as she realized what he was doing, showing her a piece of his sculpture. Like she'd shown him her pictures.

She set the computer on the bed and went to the dresser with the wrought iron framed mirror. Lowering her gaze, she lost her breath. She carefully picked up the foot-high piece, lifting it to the afternoon light streaming through her window. Stunning and heartbreaking. A soldier forced to one knee by the weight of his rifle over his shoulder. The absolute weariness in the man, the heaviness of the rifle, symbolized the burden of responsibility and duty.

The image was so powerful and compelling she couldn't get her breath. Gently, she turned it one way and another to examine every line and nuance. Finally, she studied the cold determination on his face. "He's going to get up again. Keep doing his job." She could see it in the set of the soldier's jaw, the way he leaned forward, trying to bear the unbearable weight he carried.

Her eyes burned and her heart squeezed. This single piece screamed of a quiet battle raging within a man. Within Hunt. The piece was as beautiful as it was disturbing. Alyssa had no idea how long she stood in the slice of sunlight, studying the sculpture, absorbing every subtlety and meaning, her fingers tracking every line that Hunt's fingers had shaped.

His story.

He'd shared that with her. Given her this part of himself that he hadn't given to anyone else. All her uncertainty fled. Holding his statue, she spun and headed to the kitchen to find him stirring spaghetti into a pot of bubbling water. Next to that was the pan of sauce he'd started when she came in from the terrace. It was the sight of his suddenly tense shoulders that pinged her chest.

He knew she'd returned. Slowly he finished his task, then faced her with distant, cautious eyes.

She carefully set the sculpture on the island. It was an effort to let go of it. Once she had, though, she rushed to him and threw her arms around his neck, hugging him.

"Whoa." He wrapped his arms around her waist and lifted her to his face.

"Thank you. You showed me a part of you, a piece of what you keep locked up. It means everything to me. That sculpture is powerful. I can't decide if I love it or hate it, but if I had the chance, I'd buy it to have forever. It's a part of who you are."

"It took me two days to choose the right piece." Hunt stroked his fingers along her hairline. "It's yours if you want it."

"You're giving it to me?"

"I want you to have something of me. Something I wouldn't give anyone else." He kept touching her, one arm around her waist, holding her off the ground, the other stroking her face.

"I've decided how I feel. I love it because it's your truth, your story. Thank you."

A smile chased out the hard lines and lingering shadows as he set her on her feet. "I did it for me. I need you to know me, to understand what I am and still not be scared of me." His eyes heated and he skimmed his knuckles down her cheek.

"I'm not scared." Instead, despite seeing the quiet agony Hunt carried in his sculpture, there was something uplifting and empowering about this man's trust. He'd shown no one else—not even his parents or Erin. "One second." Alyssa picked up the sculpture.

"Where are you going?"

"I'm putting this in my room." She quickly put it by her bed, and then returned.

He arched a brow. "Afraid I'll change my mind?"

She grinned at him. "No, I want your full attention on me when I say this." She didn't want him looking at that statue and thinking that he was not good enough to touch her.

"That right?"

She took a breath. "You wanted me to wait a day or two, and I have. So here it is. This right now? It's an escape, a moment in time where I'm out of the media spotlight and I can do this for me. Be selfish." She put her hand on his chest, feeling his strong heartbeat through his T-shirt. "I'm asking you to kiss me."

Hunt turned, his back rippling as he clicked off the gas flame beneath the noodles and sauce. When he faced her again, all the doubt had left his face.

The change was so sudden, she asked, "What are you doing?"

He stalked toward her, intensity burning in his eyes. "What did I say would happen if you asked me to kiss you again?"

Her mouth dried, her pulse danced a sensual beat. She reached out, slapping her hand down on the counter. In seconds, he'd turned this on her. She thought she was the aggressor, but he took control. And she liked it. "You won't stop at a kiss."

A wolfish grin spread over his face. "You sure you're ready?" He caught her arms, pulling her against all six feet of hard, warm male. "I've been controlling myself every damned second."

He held her easily, giving her a glimpse of his need. His breath feathered over her face.

"If you say yes, then you're giving yourself to me right here, right now. For this moment in time, you're mine."

Excitement buzzed in her veins. If she said the word, he'd unleash the power he'd been holding back. No fear, just them. "Yes."

Hunt scooped her up, crossed a few steps, and set her on the barstool. "God, I've ached to kiss you again." Sinking his fingers into her hair, he tilted her head and brushed his lips over hers. Then he plunged in, his tongue demanding entrance.

Latching onto his shoulders, she kissed him back, tangling her tongue with his. Alyssa lost herself to the sensation of

Hunt owning her mouth. Her lips throbbed in time with her wild pulse. Nothing had ever felt like this. So real and raw, an agonizing want burning between them.

Spreading his hand over her lower back, he wedged between her thighs and tugged her into the hard ridge of his erection. He dragged his mouth along her jaw and down her throat, making her shiver. In just minutes, she burned. Needed. His lips scorched a trail to her shoulder. Desire heated her belly. He was giving her what she wanted, craved. "Wait."

Lifting his head, he locked stare on her. "Second thoughts?"

Softening his hold on her lower back, he stroked her skin as if soothing her. That action swelled her heart and desire. Hunt had made her come at the cliffs and now he was rock hard for her, and if she said no…he'd stop. That made her want him more. "No." She pushed his shirt up. "I want to touch you." She ran her hands over the ridges of his stomach, feeling his muscles jerk. "Please."

Reaching over his head, he grabbed a handful of his shirt, yanked it off, and tossed it on the counter.

She ran her gaze over his incredible inked shoulders and chest, catching sight of a bullet tattoo over his heart. Odd. She'd ask later. Right now, she molded her hands over the thickness of his shoulders, absorbing and memorizing the feel of him. Tracing the warm skin of his chest, and wrapping her hands around the bands of muscle on the sides of his abs then back to the front to that thin trail of hair leading down.

His muscles undulated and he hissed in sharply.

She glanced up. Color bloomed in his face, and his eyes burned. She undid the button on his shorts, eased down his zipper. His massive erection sprang out, long and thick.

Alyssa traced the darker colored head, entranced by the soft feel. Wrapping her fingers around him, she pushed down his hard length.

Hunt shuddered, his thighs and abs visually rippling.

A hot sense of power roared in her ears. Her touch did this to him. Experimenting, she stroked the sensitive tip with one palm while jacking him with her fingers.

Hunt slammed his palm down on the counter. Thrusting into her hand, he leaned toward her. "Kiss me."

She looked up and he sealed his mouth over hers.

• • •

She was trying to kill him. Jesus, he loved it. Her hand on his cock drove him to the edge, but her mouth? The way she opened to him wet and hot ripped down his spine. More, he wanted more of her and sucked in her bottom lip, then thrust his tongue against hers, absorbing the taste of her. So damned perfect.

Instinctively, she matched his fierceness, stroking his cock harder, kissing him deeper, ripping away the last of his control. She stripped him raw. His orgasm hovered so close, he shuddered. Sheer will held it off.

Breaking the kiss, he eased her hand off his dick and swept her up in his arms. "Need a condom, they're in my room." His heart pounded and he struggled to breathe beneath the searing heat and anticipation. "Then it's my turn. Your clothes are coming off, and I'm going to touch you, kiss you and drive my cock into you while looking into your eyes." He swallowed a deep groan at just the thought of thrusting into her heat. He took a step, determined not to stumble. Lyssie trusted him for sex and to keep her safe. "I can't wait. Have to—"

The front door banged open. "Where is she? Where is the runaway bride trending all over social media?"

"Fuck." Hunt snarled. In the space of a second he set Lyssie down, zipped up his shorts, and leaned his forehead against hers. "I'm going to kill my sister."

Alyssa stared up at him with unfocused eyes. "Erin always did know how to make an entrance."

Chapter Eight

Hunt couldn't believe his sister showed up now. Why the hell had he ever given Erin the codes to his alarm system? His entire body and mind burned for Lyssie, craved her in a way that went beyond sex. When he touched her, the darkness inside him, the one that drove him to his studio to vent his nightmares, pulled back. He dragged in a breath of regret and stepped back from Lyssie just as his sister blew in like a summer storm, full of wild wheat curls and boundless energy.

Erin skidded to a stop in front of them with furious eyes. "How long have you two been together?" She turned to Alyssa on the barstool. "All these years, I don't hear from you. Nothing. And now you're sleeping with my brother?"

Alyssa cringed back. "Erin, no, it's not like that."

An icy wind blew over Hunt's lust. "We're not together." Not like that. They weren't in a relationship. This was an agreement, one where no one got hurt.

Lyssie stood. "I hired Hunt and his agency to help me

with a problem."

"Really?" Erin shoved her hand in her purse and pulled out her phone. "Because this picture on RevealPop doesn't look like a working relationship to me." She thumbed through her phone, then turned it toward them.

Lyssie stiffened at the mention of the tabloid journalism site. They both leaned in to see a full-color picture of Alyssa sitting on Hunt's lap at the cliffs, the two of them locked in a searing, intimate kiss.

"Oh God." She jerked back, wrapping her arms around herself in a protective gesture. "It wasn't a gun you saw, it was a camera. I haven't even announced my breakup with Nate yet."

"Looks like social media did it for you," Erin said. "Twitter has blown up with 'runaway bride' hashtags. And some that are less than flattering."

All the color drained from Lyssie's face. "Eli. Nate will hear about the picture. What if he does something else to him?"

Hunt caught her upper arms, cutting off her escalating panic. "Griff and his team are watching the boy 24/7. He's safe. No one can get to him."

She calmed, tugging her arms free. "All right, thank you."

Before his eyes she deflated. This was his fault. He should never have kissed her out there. Hell, he'd done more than kiss her. Shit, there could be other, worse pictures out there. What the hell had he been thinking? It was his job to protect her, not expose her like this. She'd been trying to avoid media attention. "I'm sorry. I'm supposed to protect you and I let this happen."

She shook her head. "I did it, I asked you to kiss me."

She turned to Erin. "I went to Hunt because I was desperate. I know it looks like I'm cheating on my fiancé with Hunt, but it's not the case. I broke up with Nate, then went to Hunt because I was scared and needed help. This…" She gestured to the phone. "Just happened."

Hunt couldn't believe how everything had gone to shit in seconds. "Lyssie—"

"I need to make some calls." She slipped between him and his sister, heading toward the hallway.

"Alyssa!" Erin called out.

She halted by the sofa and looked back.

The anger and frustration had drained from his sister. Now she appeared confused. "Who's Eli?"

Hunt tensed, ready to tell Erin to back off.

Lyssie closed her eyes, then opened them. "He's my son." Then she was gone.

Hunt ran a hand over his face. "Goddamnit." He snatched his phone out of his pocket and saw a dozen missed text messages and voicemails. He'd set it on vibrate earlier today after finally deciding which statue to show Lyssie.

He'd shared a part of his darkness with her and she'd still wanted him, trusted him, just like she'd trusted him at the cliffs, and he'd failed her.

Erin put her hand on his arm. "Alyssa has a son?"

He met his sister's eyes. "She gave him up for adoption at birth. It wasn't long after her mom died. Her ex is threatening her and the boy to force her to marry him. That's why she ran to me for help."

Erin's face blanched. "Damn."

"Yeah."

She peered up at him. "You care about Alyssa."

He gripped the edge of the counter and met his sister's eyes. "I shouldn't touch her. I'm too damaged."

Erin popped her butt up on the counter and swung her legs. "Didn't look like she was fighting you off in that picture. Or when I walked in tonight. I don't even want to know why your shirt is balled up on the counter."

Hunt glanced at his T-shirt, regret digging in. Lyssie was so damned giving and trusting, and he hadn't protected her. It crawled up his spine, tightening his jaw. "She's lonely."

His sister snorted. "Yeah. The rich, beautiful heiress that rocks the cover of every magazine is so lonely that you're her only choice for a hookup." She glared at him. "I was her best friend, you think I don't know she had it bad for you?"

Hunt crossed his arms. "I've changed."

Worry shadowed her eyes. "Yeah, you have. You came home with scars, Hunt. We all know it."

"I'm dealing with it." That's why he needed his studio. Art was the only way he could give voice to his nightmares.

She nodded. "So yeah, you changed, but one thing hasn't." Erin leaned closer. "You're the one Alyssa ran to. After all these years, Hunt, it was you. It's always been you."

Stunned, he snapped upright. Erin had a point. When Lyssie had been truly scared and out of options, she had run to him.

"The question is, can you let go of your ghosts and grab on to your chance for something special? Or do you want to spend the rest of your life holed up in a locked room wishing you'd had the guts to try?"

• • •

"Some bastard took a picture of you in a private moment and sold it to a tabloid. Don't you get sick of that crap? They should be arrested for sneaking around and invading your privacy."

Alyssa had calmed down in the last couple hours. Hunt called Griff then handed Alyssa the phone. The man had assured her Eli and his family were fine, no problems. Then Erin had burst into her bedroom, and the next thing Alyssa knew, she was spilling her guts, telling Erin about her baby and what happened with Nate.

Now she was tired of talking about herself. The lighted pool shimmered in the soft night as she and Erin sat with their legs dangling in the warm water. "Um, speaking of invasions, you barged in tonight because you saw the picture."

"That's different. Hunt never changed the locks, and he gave me his alarm codes to keep an eye on the house when he's not here." She scrunched her nose and glared across the pool. "The only code he won't give me is to the studio."

"And you haven't cracked it yet?"

"No, damn it."

Erin was still the same, and God she had missed her.

"I can't believe he gave you one of his sculptures. He hasn't shown anyone."

She leaned against Erin's shoulder. "I'm safer. Hunt loves you guys too much. My opinion isn't as important to him."

"You're wrong. He trusts you with this part of him that he can't trust with us. That's huge, Alyssa."

Her stomach warmed at the idea that she might be able to help Hunt a little bit. That she'd leave him with something more than just memories of sex with her. Speaking of that,

"You're really not mad at me anymore for kissing Hunt?" They'd done more than kiss, but Erin didn't need the details.

"I was hurt, not mad. You were my best friend, Alyssa, then you pushed us out of your life. And I get it now, well, as much as I can without having actually been through what you had." She paused and added, "Don't hurt Hunt. I know what Rachel did after that mall shooting." Erin compressed her mouth. "She hurt my brother after he saved her and a lot of other people's lives that day."

"Why didn't you kick her ass?"

"I would have, but I didn't want her to go to the media and tell them Hunt's name. I'm not sure how he managed to keep his identity quiet, but he never wanted that spotlight on him."

Oh. Worry poured back into her. "Crap, that picture could bring the spotlight down on him."

Erin's shoulder bumped her. "Let's not do this tonight. Hunt's letting you in, and he gave you that sculpture. You're reaching him when no one else could. You're safe here from your asshole ex, and he can't get to the kid either. We need to celebrate and have fun." She lowered her eyes. "My bikini looks good on you. Hunt's going to lose his mind when he sees you in that. Now let's see if we can get him to let loose a little bit."

More than ready for a break from the constant tension, she asked, "How?"

"Remember when we used to practice our dance moves out here?"

That made her grin. "Your mom danced with us too."

"Hunt and my dad would pick us up and spin us around and around until we were dizzy."

Alyssa climbed to her feet. "Or Hunt would *accidently* let go, tossing us in the pool."

Erin turned on the music and grabbed Alyssa's hand.

As the music flowed around them, along with the scent of grapes and pool water, her worries fell away.

. . .

Hunt damn near fell into the pool. He'd finished his phone call, making the arrangements for a surprise for Lyssie. After he changed into his board shorts, he came outside to music blasting. His gaze barely slid over his sister before locking onto Lyssie—her head thrown back, hair swinging as she danced with total abandon.

Stopping before he tumbled over the pool edge into the water, he got an eyeful of a criminally tiny bikini top barely covering her breasts. His mouth watered and his hands itched to mold and shape those small mounds, then draw that top down and expose her nipples. Would they be dark with tight little points?

She twisted around and light shimmered off the pale skin of her stomach with the gentle swell of her hips. His attention caught on her small heart tattoo with the tear center, the tail of the heart dipping into the wisp of black material masquerading as bikini bottoms. They barely covered her and were cut so high on her thighs it would just take a nudge of his fingers...

Or tongue...

Stop. Jesus. He tried to close his eyes, but his lids weren't cooperating. God he wanted her. Was desperate to be inside her, feeling her heat spasm around him as she lost control for him. And he'd be right there with her, coming hard enough to forget his own name. The need pounded deep in his spine.

Lyssie erupted in laughter, the rich sound rolling over his skin like a caress. Sensual fire burned in her as she let herself go…just danced. He fisted his hands to keep from yanking her against his body to feel every inch of her flaming beauty sliding against him. His blood thundered and his heart pounded with a blazing need to have her.

Not just her body, but the essence of her that burned away the ice caging him. There was such hope in her, the way she viewed the world with a rare optimism even though she'd been through dark shit. All he had to do was recall her pictures to know that view was her truth. Where Hunt saw potential ambushes and death, Lyssie saw hope and love.

She drew him like no one else ever had.

Another laugh rolled through him, torturing his cock and maybe his soul.

Hunt dragged in a gulp of air and ordered his body to stand down. Now. He'd trained to have absolute control.

His body gave him the finger as heat licked his nerve endings.

"There you are," his sister yelled out. "Come dance with us."

If he got within touching distance of Lyssie… Nope. "I'll swim." He dove into the pool and swam a few laps, trying to cool off. Finally he headed to the shallow end, braced his arms on the deck. "You two tire yourselves out yet?"

"Nope, but I'm thirsty." Erin grabbed the two bottles of water.

Lyssie faced him and smirked. "We're young, we don't tire out like an old man."

Erin laughed. "He turned thirty this year. Probably gets worn out just thinking about dancing."

"Thirty!" Turning, she gave him a pitying look. "Will you need help getting out of the pool?"

With his hands on the deck, he leaped out of the water and started toward the troublemakers. "That's three, princess."

Lyssie's eyes widened and she lowered the water bottle. "Three what?"

"Times you've smarted off. Lucky for you the pool's nice and warm." He stalked toward her.

She spun, slapped down her water bottle and launched into a run.

She was fast, her runner's muscles rippling down her thighs and calves, but he was faster. Hunt sprang, catching her before she got to the house, and easily sweeping her up into his arms. Her warm skin pressed against his as he strode to the pool. "Do I feel old to you now?"

"Put me down!" Squirming and laughing at the same time, she tried to push against his chest.

He reached the edge of the pool and jumped in while holding her.

Erin followed them in to save Lyssie. Hunt laughed and tossed his sister across the pool. It was on. The two girls spent an hour trying to tackle him. When they tired, Hunt leaned back in the shallow end while the girls sat on the edge of the pool.

Erin blurted out, "Alyssa said she'd do a tribute video for Mom and Dad's award dinner as a surprise from you and me."

Hunt raised his eyebrows. "Lyssie's doing all the work, and we're taking the credit? Did you twist her arm?" Erin could be very persuasive.

"Actually, I offered. I'd love to do it if you don't mind. I'll need to get interviews with both of you."

The pool lights reflected off her flushed skin and bright eyes, yet her fingers clutching the edge of the pool were white knuckled. As if she feared his answer. "It's a great idea. They'll be thrilled."

He turned his attention to his sister. "Did you tell Lyssie about your show in New York?" He was so damned proud of his sister.

"New York?" Alyssa's face flooded with happiness. "Oh my God, Erin, that's huge! Tell me everything."

Erin described the upcoming event and the pieces she planned to show, then ended with, "Will you come, Alyssa? You and Hunt can come together."

"Oh, I'd love to." Her uncertain gaze collided with his, then she jerked it away. "But I'll come on my own. By then, my problems with Nate will be resolved and Hunt will move on to his next job."

That brought him up short. Was that what she thought? She was just a job? *That's what you told her. Oh sure you're not letting her pay you, but you told her that you'd only screw her while you're her bodyguard.*

Was he really any different from everyone else who used her?

• • •

Alyssa cleaned up the patio, throwing away water bottles and laying towels out to dry while Hunt walked his sister out to her car. Done with that, she went to the wrought iron table and pulled out her camera to look at the shots she'd gotten tonight.

She heard the sliding door open. Her skin tightened and her pulse skipped. *Hunt.* Was he coming out to talk to her, or to go in his studio and lock her out?

Or did he want to finish what Erin interrupted earlier?

Needing some way to get control of the sensation that was careening out of control, she switched her camera to video and watched him in the display window as he strode toward her. The pool lights danced off his sandy hair and dark tats streaked over his shoulders and biceps. It made her happy to capture them on video, where the fluidity of the lines would show better than a picture.

Hunt stopped but Alyssa moved around him, getting a close-up on the script of one bicep then the other. "Stay still."

"Hey, you're the cover girl, not me."

"Quiet, I'm working here."

"Is that right?" He pivoted until he faced her. "In your bikini?"

"That's the beauty of being behind the camera. It doesn't matter what I wear."

"Oh, it matters to me."

His voice had pitched low, trembling in her chest and belly. Alyssa homed in on the one tat she'd seen for the first time earlier tonight. Holding the camera with one hand, she traced the bullet inked over his heart. "Why?"

His eyes shadowed. "Superstition. It was my first tat."

"What does it signify?"

"The bullet meant to kill me. If I have it, then another sniper doesn't."

A shiver forced her to pull her hand back to hold the camera steady. Something shifted in her head, and adrenaline flooded her veins. "Did you want to be a sniper?"

He backed up a step, sliding onto a barstool. "Are you interviewing me?"

"Yep."

"For?"

Alyssa lowered the camera, pausing the video. This was the man who'd shared one of his sculptures with her. She wanted to tell him about her website. Would he laugh at her? Think it silly and a waste of time like Nate and Parker? *Be brave.* "It's my dream."

He arched a brow. "To interview me?"

"There's that ego again." She rolled her eyes. "I meant finding out people's stories. Not famous people, but real people. Like Treva, she's incredible. And there are so many more like her. Some I do in still shots, others I do videos with my voice over. I would love to get stories like the man who owns the taco stand. Surviving a roadside bomb, that can't be easy, but he does it. Maybe when I get my life sorted out, I can talk to him, see if he'd be open to the idea."

Hunt leaned back, stretching one arm along the bar. "This is what you've been working on."

She wanted him to know. "I'm working on a website to launch soon. It's called Streets of Valor. Getting stories in a picture or video of people who overcome adversity or do incredible things." Passion burned in her chest.

Hunt went absolutely still. "Don't put me on your site."

Is that what he thought? "I never do that without permission. I always get signed releases. I know what it feels like to be exposed that way, like the picture of us that's out there now." Dropping her eyes to her camera, she added, "This was just for me."

"All right, ask me a question."

Her doubt cleared and she restarted her video. "So did you want to become a sniper?" She'd known he'd wanted to be a Marine, but not a sniper.

Hunt shifted, leaning an elbow on his thigh. "Yes. I thought I would track down the worst mass murderers, the men who strapped bombs to children, sent them into a crowd and killed dozens. Men who masterminded flying airplanes into buildings full of innocents."

The intensity rolling off him and the way his eyes looked right into the camera gave her chills. This was the kind of reality few people would ever encounter in their lives. "Did you?"

"I absolutely saved countless lives. I became the Nightmare Ghost Hunter that terrorists around the world feared, but there's always a cost. Killing changes a man, and it's all too easy to become the very thing you kill."

The truth of that sliced into her. "But you didn't."

"No. I left before that happened. And every day here at home, I keep a careful lock on that part of me. The killer."

His honesty stunned her. "Is that really what they called you? Nightmare Ghost Hunter?"

Hunt reached out, taking the camera from her and turning it off. "You pull more out of me than anyone else." He cupped his warm hands around her hips. "I never talk about this."

She liked that he talked to her and wanted to reassure him. "No one will see this unless you want to share it some-day, maybe with your family." A sense of power filled her.

Not cruel power like Nate tried to exert over her, but the power to help the man she cared about. "If you trust me, I can show you what you look like through my eyes. I understand that you were a sniper, but that was one part of the bigger picture of who you are." A courageous, honorable man who deserved to love and to be loved.

He rubbed his thumbs over her hip bones. "Do you have any idea what you're doing to me right now, showing me what you really love? Owning your passion about your website? That's hot, baby."

He found her sexy like this? Her pulse danced all over the place, blood rushed in her ears. Every brush of his fingertips shot straight to her nipples. Need pooled in her belly. It happened so fast, she could barely breathe.

"Drying hair tumbling around you, that ridiculous excuse for a bikini clinging to your breasts, outlining your stiff nipples." His eyes rose to hers. "Begging for my hands and mouth."

Hot intensity rolled off him. Her nipples tightened to the point of pain, crazed for his touch. Alyssa couldn't move, frozen to the spot beneath his sizzling scrutiny.

"I want you, Lyssie, exactly as you are now, wild, free, not holding back from me or yourself. I'm not taking you into my bedroom, shutting off the lights and having polite sex."

Nothing they'd done together yet had been polite and she wanted more. Streaks of heat traveled to her core and clenched hard. She dug her fingers into the thick muscles of his shoulders. "I don't want polite sex." She wanted this. Them.

"I've got one thin thread of control left. *One.* I've had a taste of you, and now I'm damn near crazed with the need to possess every inch of you. No holding back. You'll give me everything, letting me kiss, touch and fuck you into screaming pleasure." Hunger glinted in his eyes. "If you've changed your mind or you're not ready, walk away. Go in the house and I'll go in my studio. But if you stay, you're mine."

Her heart stuttered. She could barely see the younger man she remembered. This man pumped out danger, protection, and primitive sexual need, but the sexiest part was that her needs were as important as his. It hit her then, he wasn't holding back either. He was letting her see him right down to his erection tenting his board shorts.

She leaned close to him. "I'm staying."

Whatever control he had snapped and he surged up, lifted her, and sat her on the padded seat of the stool. Before she could adjust, he crashed his mouth to hers. He took possession, sliding his tongue against hers. With his hand in her hair, he tilted her head back and took the kiss deeper. Brushing the tip of his tongue along the roof of her mouth sent wild tingles through her.

Alyssa forgot to breathe, could only feel. Heart pounding and blood rushing, she dug her fingers into his thick shoulders.

Dragging his mouth from hers, he stared into her eyes. "I want to see you." Hunt lifted his fingers to her nape where her top was tied. "No one is here, just us. I made sure of it by electronically locking down the gate to the property." He narrowed his eyes. "You're for my eyes only."

She believed him, trusted him.

Drawing it down, his gaze locked onto her breasts.

The cool air hit her damp skin with vivid awareness.

Would he be disappointed? She'd definitely been in the small stack line in the boob department.

"Beautiful. So damned perfect." He tossed her top to the bar and cupped her, rubbing his thumbs over the turgid tips.

Hot streaks arced right to her core, making her squirm. She tried to sit still, not wanting him to stop.

His eyes narrowed. "Tell me."

The growl in his voice ripped away another layer of resistance. "Don't stop."

"This?" He rolled them, firing a blazing trail to her womb.

"Oh God." Her lower stomach clenched. Sizzled. She couldn't sit still. "Yes. It's never enough."

"Good girl." Hot approval rode those words. He sank into her mouth and kept up his sensual assault on her breasts, then kissed a path to her ear and whispered, "I'm going to lick your sweet nipples, then graze them with my teeth." He tweaked the already tender buds just enough.

A sound she didn't recognize spilled from her throat. A plea. Her breasts were a fast track to her libido, and he'd cared enough to figure that out.

"Oh yeah, you like hearing what I'm going to do to you, as much as I liked you demanding to touch me earlier." He skated one hand down her belly, circling her belly button, then dropped it to her thigh and drew his fingers up and up.

Chill bumps chased his touch.

He licked the shell of her ear, then down over the curve of her jaw. Too many sensations. "Hunt." She clung to his shoulders. Outside, with the pool lights shimmering their watery glow, she watched as he skated his mouth to her nipple and dragged his wet, slightly rough tongue over a distended tip.

Lightning arrowed straight down. Hunt wedged his hips between her legs, his thick erection brushing her inner thigh through his board shorts. Leaning in, he teased her nipple with the lightest edge of his teeth. She couldn't bear it and sank her fingers into his hair, holding him to her.

"My brave, sexy girl. You take my breath away, then give it back with every sigh or moan." He edged his fingers up to the top of her bikini bottoms. "Use my shoulders. Lift up."

More excitement flared at the thought of him stripping her bare. He tugged the bottoms off, then he was back, his hands on her thighs gently spreading her open to his perusal. Heat rushed through her veins and her heart pounded in her ears.

"When I see you like this, sharing yourself with me, you're the light that's been missing in my world. Pretty, yet powerful enough to bring me to my knees."

The look on his face was like nothing she'd seen before and it filled the part of her starved to be accepted and cherished.

Hunt brushed the pad of his finger over her nub then down to her folds, and back up. His harsh face darkened with dusky color as he teased her cleft with feathery strokes. Bracing an arm behind her back, he said, "Lean back. I have you."

She rested against his powerful arm.

Hunt covered one of her nipples with his mouth the exact second one long finger penetrated her, gliding past her sensitized wall. He circled his thumb around her aching clit, ramping up her desire, setting a pace of in and out with his finger, round and round with his thumb, all while licking, sucking her nipples.

Riotous sensations erupted. Never had she been so vividly aware of her body and desire. Pleasure built and Alyssa dropped her head back, giving herself to the feel of him. His hot, wet mouth, his long, knowing fingers. Every stroke sent lightning whips. Tension tightened. Alyssa gasped as her orgasm detonated. So powerful, she cried out.

Hunt tugged her against his chest, his fingers stroking her as he said in a rough growl, "Next one will be when I'm thrusting deep inside you, feeling you squeeze my cock as we both lose control."

That sent another wave of pleasure rippling through her.

Chapter Nine

Something snapped inside him. A need so fierce, Hunt obeyed it blindly.

He had to get inside Lyssie—make her his.

He couldn't hold back, the drive pounded mercilessly. Holding her with one arm, he shoved down his board shorts, his engorged, eager cock springing out. Once he kicked them away, he fisted her tangled hair and eased her head back. Her eyelids fluttered, pupils swollen. She'd given him that gift, coming for him without reserve. "I need you. This." The words scraped up his throat.

He wasn't in control. He knew it. Didn't care. Not when it was with her, his Lyssie. Joining their mouths, he tasted the half a glass of wine she'd had out by the pool, and that sweeter vanilla flavor that was all her.

Lyssie skimmed her hands down his sides to his hips and stroked her thumbs in the hollows of his hip bones, driving him mad, shooting streaks of heat to his balls. The soft skin of her inner thighs brushed his hips, fueling his compulsion to bury himself inside her. Tugging her forward on the stool, he guided the swollen tip against her entrance.

The warm slick feel of her bathing his sensitized head combined with her tiny gasp as he pushed in shot down his back. Hunt surged into her. With one hand on her back to brace her, he lost his mind in the blazing hot feel of her molten walls closing around him.

Nothing in his life had ever felt like this.

He pulled out, thrust in, and took her mouth, licking in deep as he plunged again—and again.

"Oh God." Her body bowed beneath his and she dug her hands in his hair.

Jerking his head back from her mouth, he took in her flushed face and unfocused gaze. So beautiful, needy, and *his*. That shoved his impending orgasm back just enough as he powered into her. "Can't hold back. Are you close?"

"Not quite. Please." She tugged on his hair, her hips bucking while urgency built in her eyes.

Her sweet begging totally undid him. Every instinct he had roared to life. Reaching between them, he slid his thumb over her clit, feeling her thighs tremble in response. A low moan spilled from her throat. She dropped her head back as her pleasure exploded. "Hunt!" It came out shrill and wild, her fingers digging into his shoulders.

Hunt drove into her and growled, his release destroying him. Savage pleasure took him apart, wave after wave. Minutes or hours later, he could barely move. Buried balls deep in Lyssie, he didn't want to leave. Heavy contentment filled his chest as he stroked her hair and the soothing sounds of the night surrounded them.

Until his gaze caught on his board shorts where he'd kicked them away.

The still-wrapped condom spilling out of the pocket.

"Oh hell."

Lyssie lifted her head. "What?"

He should be more panicked, more freaked, but her skin was flushed and her eyes soft, easing that flare of worry trying to ignite in his stomach. He ran his fingers down her spine, feeling her body flutter around his dick from his touch. "I forgot to use a condom." That never happened. Except with Lyssie.

"Oh. I didn't think of it either."

That flicker of tension returned.

She stroked his shoulder and biceps, tracing a finger over his tat. "But I should be safe. I timed my last birth control shot to last until…" A tiny frown gathered between her eyebrows. "That is, I should be covered for another couple weeks."

He leaned his forehead against hers. She hadn't wanted to mention her wedding, none of that outside shit belonged here with them. "This is what you do to me, drive me to lose my mind. But we're using condoms from now on." The last thing he wanted was a kid, or to leave Lyssie pregnant and alone.

· · ·

"Morning."

Alyssa opened her eyes to see Hunt's bedroom. She lay on her side, her back to his front, his arms around her. "I fell asleep with you." She couldn't believe she'd done that. The

last thing she wanted was him worrying about her under-
standing this was just sex. For him anyway. "I meant to go
back to my room."

"I wanted you here." His voice was morning rough and
sexy. Hunt pressed his hand to her belly, tracing her tat then
touching the tear suspended in the middle. "What does it
mean?"

Turning her head, she got the full impact of Hunt loom-
ing over her. "It's a dragon tear."

Gently brushing it, he kept his eyes on her. "What's it
for? You don't have any other tats. This means something."

"Are you interviewing me, Marine?"

"Not on camera. No way in hell would I let anyone else
see what I'm seeing."

"What's that?"

"The real Alyssa Brooks, naked and uncensored in my
bed and hot as hell." He leaned closer. "The woman I let
interview me on tape and trust not to let that get out."

That humbled her. Hunt had trusted her to capture
him on her camera and not expose his dark struggles to the
world. Shifting to her back, she laid her hand over his resting
on her belly. "This is where I carry Eli. I gave him up, but I
won't forget him. I loved him so much, Hunt. I didn't want
to let him go." In a blink, she was back in that hospital room,
her baby boy in her arms. So tiny, fragile and beautiful. Love
had overwhelmed her, nearly crushing her.

"Do you regret it, Lyssie?"

His words pulled her back. "I regret that I failed him,
failed to be the mother he deserved, but I did the right thing
for him. I was too young and broken."

He flipped his hand, threading their fingers. "You didn't

break."

"Almost." She was done hiding. "I'd been pretty spoiled and sheltered my whole life, and suddenly at seventeen, I was pregnant and scared. Then the accident that killed my mom and…" She wasn't sure how to describe it. "Remember that song 'Tears of the Dragon' by Bruce Dickinson?"

He nodded, stroking his thumb over hers where their hands were joined. "You loved it when I had it playing in the studio."

Every touch of his fingers reached deeper inside her. "That's how I felt, stumbling in the dark, tears I couldn't cry choking and drowning me. I had this inked with the tear red for the piece of my heart that my son will always own." She swallowed the emotion building in her throat. "I gave him up, but I will never stop loving him."

With his arm beneath her shoulders he pulled her to him. "You've never cried? My girl who used to cry at commercials?"

He'd always teased her about that, his whole family had. "Before I had him, yes, but that morning, I couldn't. I didn't dare. I'd have truly broken and I refused to do that. What if he needed me at some point? Or wants to find me when he's an adult?"

Hunt cupped her face. "That's strong, and I'm damned proud of you. You made a hard choice not for yourself, but for your son."

"I hope so. Mark and Janis seemed like people who would love him. I hope I chose right." She believed they were what her boy needed.

"I have something for you."

The shift in subjects had her struggling to catch up. "We just woke up. When—"

"*You* just woke up. My phone woke me a while ago." He reached back and picked up his cell. "It's a video."

"Of what? Wait, is this about the picture that was in the media yesterday?" As upset as she'd been, there was nothing she could do about it. It was out.

"No. Yesterday, you were so worried about Eli after that picture of us kissing went viral, I asked Griff to see if he could get permission from Eli's parents to do a short video of him for you."

Her gaze latched onto the sleek black phone in his hand. "You have one?" She couldn't quite get her breath as ferocious longing to see Eli clawed at her. She shoved up to a sitting position.

Hunt sat next to her. "It's only a few minutes long. Do you want to watch it alone?"

Alyssa pressed her sweaty palms together, excitement and anxiety colliding in her belly. "No." She didn't want him to leave her. All those times she got that once-a-year email with a picture and a few quick details of his life she'd been alone. No one to share that moment with, to talk about how he had her mom's eyes, or that he was getting so big. No one with whom to share the child who had changed her in significant ways. "Will you watch it with me?"

He wrapped his arm around her and pulled her close. "Ready?"

No. Yes. She didn't know so she nodded her head, eyes fixed on the screen of his phone. In seconds, everything else slid away as she watched the slender boy with brown hair and long legs chasing a soccer ball. He had on tan shorts and a T-shirt.

Eli stopped the soccer ball, jumped over it, and kicked it

in the other direction.

Alyssa leaned forward, drinking him in as the camera zoomed in. His hair was lighter than hers, his eyes had some green like her mom's had, and he laughed. "I did it!"

A tall bald man strode into the scene and scooped the boy up in his big hands. "You're going to be better than me soon."

Pride filled Eli's eyes and he hugged the man.

"Doesn't mean you can beat Mom." Janis walked up to them carrying the ball, her face beaming. "Let's do this, boys." She dropped the ball and kicked it.

Marcus put Eli down and a couple minutes later they were all laughing and struggling to steal the ball. In the last scene, Janis tripped, going to her knees. Eli forgot the ball, racing to his mom and hugging her. Janis lifted her eyes to the camera as she wrapped the boy in her arms and mouthed two simple words. *Thank you.*

The video ended.

Her eyes filled and nothing could stop the storm of tears, the collision of happiness and grief.

Hunt pulled her onto his lap, holding her close. "Let go, baby. I know it hurts, it's okay to cry." He kissed her hair. "But know this, you made the right choice out of love."

• • •

Hunt rested his arm on the kitchen island and eyed Sienna on his laptop's Skype connection. "What have you found?"

The other woman leaned back in her chair. "I've talked to both Alyssa's former assistants, and they insist they were not spying on her for Madden."

"Do you believe them?"

Sienna snorted. "No. But I'm sure he paid in cash and there's no way to trace it now. Both of them were at work when we think someone got into Alyssa's house under the guise of a dress delivery. They're a dead end."

Hell. "What about the guy in Arizona that tampered with the car?"

"James Frye. Local mechanic with a record. His story is he was looking for his lost dog."

"Under the car at four a.m.?" Hunt took a drink of his coffee.

"Yep. The cops haven't found any money trail, so if he's been paid it's cash."

Shit. "Madden's had the kid watched for a while and likely has a contact there handling this. He's been careful to keep his hands clean, ensuring there are as few ties to him as possible by having others do his dirty work for him." Hunt wanted answers to find a way to neutralize Nate as a threat to Lyssie, but he didn't want this case to end because then he'd lose her.

"Yeah, but he might have done his own dirty work in the past. I got the police report on Lorelei Madden's death. Time of death was around eleven thirty at night, the assumption is she was asleep, got up to go downstairs for some reason and fell. Her son found her the next morning when he went by for their Sunday morning breakfast. His 911 call was logged in at 8:52 a.m. The scene appeared to be an accident, but the neighbor, an older gentleman, told the cops to look at the son. Said Lorelei was becoming increasingly afraid of him."

The back of his neck tingled straight down his spine. "And?"

"Autopsy said death was from the fall. Plus Madden's alibi checked out. He spent the night at his girlfriend Tami Nash's apartment. She said they were watching a movie at eleven thirty." Sienna raised her eyebrows over her glasses. "I talked to the police detective. He wasn't convinced the fall was an accident, and the fact that Madden benefited from a substantial life insurance policy added to the suspicion. There just wasn't enough evidence to make an arrest and the girlfriend stuck to her story. I'm going to get Adam to follow up with her, see if she still sticks to her story."

"Adam?" Now his boss, Adam Waters, was involved in the case.

"Alyssa's high profile and I've been keeping him up to date. He offered to take this witness since you need to protect the client and we thought Miss Nash might need someone with more tact than Cooper."

He started to agree when a new voice interrupted. "Hunt?"

He snapped his head up. Alyssa walked toward him wearing tiny shorts and holding her phone, strain weighing down her beautiful face. He surged up and reached her in two strides. "What?"

"A text." She held out her phone.

He took it from her cold fingers and read the screen. *You can't hide. And you've just shown the entire world you're a classless slut. No wonder you got knocked up at seventeen. That ends now. I expect you to be home and ready to call a news conference Monday morning at which time you'll explain that you got cold feet and made a terrible mistake that you regret. The wedding is on and we will be married. Don't be a problem. I may not be able to get to the kid, but I can always get to you or anyone else I choose. You piss me off any more and you'll pay in ways you never imagined.*

Rage slammed into his chest. He set the phone down to work on tracking it later, but Madden would be smart enough to use a burner. He wrapped his arm around Lyssie. "Has he ever called you a slut before?" Hunt really needed to get his hands on this guy.

"No, but he always said I was no better than common actresses and needed to remember it."

He didn't like that shit. "Your mother was an actress."

She nodded. "He admired her. Thought she was smart to use a few lucky breaks to build an empire."

"Lucky breaks?" That really ticked him off. "Your mother was a child actress who—"

She held up her hand. "I know the story, but if she hadn't landed that key role, *Cry for Melissa,* as an adult, her career would probably have faded away like so many other child actresses. Instead, it sent her into a rare level of stardom and then she did what she really loved, writing and producing. Nate didn't disparage my mother, he pushed me to be exactly like her." She narrowed her eyes. "I'm not my mother, and she wouldn't want this for me, I know that. I'm not letting Nate or Parker do this to me."

Hunt pulled her closer. "Parker still trying to get you to talk to him?"

"Yes. Frantic texts and emails that Dragon Wing needs me and I can't just walk away. I'm being selfish and if I come back they can explain. He refuses to believe that Nate's dangerous."

"We're taking Madden down, Lyssie. It's going to take time, but he's going to end up doing something stupid and plant his own ass in prison. You need to know we're looking at his mother's death." He tugged her into the kitchen and showed her Sienna on the laptop. Hunt got some coffee while Si filled her in.

"So what now? I can't hide forever. I won't. I quit Dragon Wing to live my own life and go after my goals, not hide."

The fire in her burned and made Hunt's hands itch to capture the absolute beauty of Lyssie breaking free and discovering her own strength, both sexually and emotionally. It was sexy, alluring and scared the hell out of him because tightly wound guys like Madden had a tendency to snap in totally unpredictable ways.

"Stay here for a while longer. Let him get back from Europe and realize he can't control you. That will put more pressure on him, and we'll see what he does. He may make a big enough mistake that we can take him down and the threat to you and Eli will end."

And so would he and Lyssie.

Chapter Ten

Alyssa ran to the beat of 'Dark Horse' by Katy Perry. She'd wound around the entire vineyard, savoring the freedom of giving herself over to the music and the run. She'd been here a week and a half and each day she felt more alive, vibrant and strong.

Beneath the beat of the music was the thump of worry. It was Monday. Nate must realize by now she wasn't doing what he demanded of her. She wasn't going back to him. What would be his next—

A horrible squeal or yelp cut over the music in her ears. Slowing her pace, she looked around. What was that? No one else was on the property except Hunt. Maybe it was a car turning a corner? Or the media? That picture all over the internet had caught the side profile of Alyssa but she'd mostly blocked Hunt's face. The media was trying to figure out who he was. Once they did, they'd swarm. Even though she didn't see any media vehicles, she turned to run up the main road to the house. Last thing she wanted was any more pictures of her on the—

Another yelping cry pitched over the music.

Her heart stuttered and chills broke out on her sweaty skin. Ripping off her earphones, she heard whimpers coming from behind her. Either a kid or an animal. The frantic cries shot adrenaline into her blood. She raced to the long gate stretched across the entrance to the vineyard. Grabbing the thick wrought iron bars, she visually searched the road. The small quiet street only had a few properties and little traffic.

There. Oh my God! A small brown and white dog lay on the road, bleeding. Someone must have hit it. Alyssa raced to the control box and jabbed the button. The gate began its slow glide to open.

She squeezed out, glanced up and down for cars, saw none and ran to the animal. Crouching down, she fought to get her panic under control. The little guy needed help. He lay on his right side, and it looked like the front left shoulder and leg were injured. Blood matted in his long fur. The dog panted and whined. "Okay, sweetheart, it's okay." Careful to avoid the injured area she stroked the dog's face.

Okay good. He didn't try to bite her, but he rolled his eyes in obvious fear.

Should she move him? Alyssa didn't know, but she couldn't leave the little guy on the road. She reached for her phone tucked into her bra top to call Hunt for help when the roar of a car engine jerked her head up.

A small truck with dark windows coming fast. Too fast.

Hot panic exploded, flinging her back in time. *The car sliding out of control, spinning wildly. The hideous crash, screeching metal, screams—*

The dog's shrill yelp yanked her from the memory to the present. The truck was closing in, dark and terrifying. She scooped up the dog, sprang up and ran. The dog howled in pain. Tears burned Alyssa's eyes. The truck tires squealed.

From her peripheral vision she saw it heading right at her. Adrenaline pumped furiously, slamming her heart against her rib cage. The truck roared closer and closer. She'd never make it.

Her body braced for impact. Oh God, oh—

Only feet from her, the truck suddenly swerved away. The engine gunned and the truck tore down the road at the same time Hunt raced out the gate, his eyes scanning up and down the street before landing on her.

"Lyssie, what happened?"

The dog shivered and whined in her arms. Her knees softened, going spongy as trembles seized her muscles. Fog filled her head and buzzed in her ears. She took a step and stumbled.

Hunt caught her elbows, steadying her. "Look at me. Tell me. Now."

His warm hands cupping her elbows and sharp words chased out her shock. "Someone tried to run me over. They swerved away just before hitting me."

• • •

Cold rage filled him. Everything snapped into hyperawareness. Getting inside the gate, he said, "Are you hurt?"

"No. The dog is. I need to get him to a vet or animal hospital."

He finally dropped his gaze to the whimpering dog. Hell. Its front left leg and shoulder were pretty banged up. He guided her to his abandoned Jeep just inside the gate and opened the passenger side door. "Sit." Once he turned off the car, he put a sterile gauze from his first aid kit on the dog's wound, then grabbed a blanket and wrapped it around both of them.

"How did you know? I mean you just showed up out of nowhere." She sucked in a choppy breath.

Hunt leaned over the dog, who'd calmed, and pulled Lyssie's face to his chest. "When you opened the gate, the alarm system alerted me. I engaged that feature after Erin surprised us Friday night. When I heard the gate opening, I knew something was wrong so I jumped in the car and raced down here. Then I saw you standing there holding the dog." She'd had an expression of confused terror on her face.

She leaned against his chest. "Thank you. I'm okay, just…adrenaline is making me shaky."

Hunt stroked her back, feeling her tremors, but his head played other images. What if he'd arrived and found her lying on the street in a pool of blood? Christ. Tugging her ponytail, he tilted her head back and looked into her eyes. "Why did you go out the gate?"

"The dog. He was hurt, crying in the street. Hit by a car, I guess."

Helpless fury roared through him. "Damn it, Lyssie, it was a set up. The dog was bait to get you out of the gate." Since she said a car tried to hit her that was the logical conclusion.

Her eyes narrowed. "I didn't know that then, but I couldn't leave him there."

"Wrong. You call me, but you don't leave this property again without me knowing it."

"You can't—"

Oh he could, because no way in hell was she putting herself in danger again. "Someone just tried to either scare you or kill you and chickened out. You'll damn well do exactly what I tell you to do."

She opened her mouth to respond when her phone beeped a message. She retrieved the phone from her shirt and looked at the screen. Her eyes widened while her lips went bloodless. "Next time, the car won't miss. Get back where you belong before someone gets hurt."

Hunt took the phone. Shit. Another blocked number.

"Nate. He did this. I didn't go home, put on his ring and call the news conference announcing we were still marrying like he demanded in that text." Her shivering increased.

Locking down his temper, he focused. "Describe the vehicle. Did you get a look at the driver?"

"Windows were tinted too dark. It happened too fast for me to see more than an older gray truck. A smaller model." She tucked the blanket around the dog, petting his head. "Do you think Nate was in that truck?"

"No. We have eyes on him. He came home from Europe Sunday morning. Tried to go to your house last night and the guards at the gate turned him away as per your instructions. I got an update a little while ago that he went into Dragon Wing this morning. Your stepfather is there too."

"He's got someone doing this, proving if he can't get to Eli he'll get to me."

"The goal is to scare you into compliance."

"Screw him." She stroked the little dog's head. "But we have to take the dog in for help. They hurt him because of me." Tears welled in her eyes.

Shit. Hunt's protective instincts battled. He wanted Lyssie safe in the house, but the dog needed help. And he wasn't leaving her alone here. "Okay. We'll take him, but we aren't staying there and waiting. I won't have you out in the open right now."

He watched logic and emotion battle it out, but finally, she nodded. "Deal. As long as I can call and get updates on the dog...and maybe I'll ask Erin to check on him so he's not alone."

Like she had been after her mom died. How had he ever thought Lyssie had turned into a rich, spoiled heiress? She'd suffered, but instead of letting it sour her, she'd become more caring.

This woman was a hell of a lot stronger than anyone had given her credit for.

• • •

Sitting on the couch in the family room, Alyssa was finishing up a Skype meeting with her wealth management team when a loud knock at the front door made her jump. Her nerves suddenly tightened. She ended the meeting, and stood as Hunt answered the door and returned, followed by a tall man with dark wavy hair and that same formidable bearing Hunt had.

Did all former Marines look so capable and sexy? Leaving her computer, she walked up to him. "Hi, I'm Alyssa Brooks."

His warm hand engulfed hers. "I'm Adam Waters, and it's a pleasure." Releasing her hand, he asked, "You holding up okay? The media shit storm is pretty brutal."

The memory of that picture being splashed all over the world made her wince internally. In the last few days it had escalated on social media, with Alyssa being called all kinds of fun names. Even better? This man was Hunt's friend, boss, and owner of Once A Marine, and he probably surmised from the photo that she was sleeping with Hunt. Taking her hand back, she kept his stare despite her embarrassment. "I'm used to it, but Hunt wasn't clearly visible in that photo, so hopefully the media will leave him alone."

Adam narrowed his eyes. "Hunt can take care of himself, but you came to us for help, not to get splashed across the media in a compromising picture."

Hunt slapped down three glasses of iced tea. "That why you insisted on coming by in person?"

The two men stared at each other, and Alyssa could feel the tension building. "Exactly." Adam sat and grabbed a cold glass.

"What's going on?" Confused, she looked up at Hunt. "I thought he talked to Nate's ex-girlfriend about the alibi. I don't understand."

Hunt tugged out a chair and gestured to it. "He could have sent a report, but Adam's here checking to make sure you're a happy client."

Which was probably a nice way of saying he was there to protect Hunt and his company. "Everything is fine. It'd be better if we could make Nate leave me alone."

Hunt dropped down in the seat next to her. "We will." He squeezed her shoulder, then turned to Adam. "What did Tami Nash say?"

Adam shook his head. "She met me on her lunch hour yesterday. She's not going to recant her statement that Nate was with her the night his mother fell down the stairs."

Alyssa stared at her glass, thinking. "Maybe he was there with her all night."

"I don't think so. The fact that she met with me tells me it's bothering her. If she does recant she could end up being disbarred for giving a false statement to police. She'd essentially be involved with a murder."

"You really think Nate killed his mother? Pushed her down the stairs?" She hadn't wanted to believe that she was sleeping with a man who could kill his own mother.

Adam measured her for long seconds. "Let me put it this way. I asked Miss Nash flat out if she was afraid of Nate Madden. She said yes."

Chills broke out on her arms. All she had to do was recall the way Nate'd pushed her against the wall in the elevator, to believe he'd have threatened his ex-girlfriend in a similar manner. "So what now?"

"Miss Nash had some things to say about Madden, including that he was obsessed with you, Alyssa. He'd constantly searched out any information on you."

Hunt set his glass of tea down. "That's the second time we've heard that."

Adam nodded. "So far, we have threats and actions we can't prove. Madden's been just careful enough, even those text messages don't trace back to him. He probably suspects he's being followed and is cautious." The man took a breath and went on. "His obsession with you, that's his breaking point. Let's pressure him, see if he does something rash. If he comes here and makes a scene, we can get him on stalking and more."

"You want to use Lyssie as bait."

She jerked at the ice in Hunt's voice. His face carved into hard unforgiving ridges.

"It's time we take control. Pressure this guy and force him to either give up or meltdown. Because my sense after talking to Miss Nash?" Adam set his heavy gaze on them both. "He's dangerous as fuck."

Fear clanged in her head. "He could go after Eli again."

Adam nodded. "The woman, Tami? She has a younger sister. Want to guess who Madden threatened? The girl was thirteen at the time. Seventeen now. Every once in a while a picture of her sister shows up in Tami's mailbox. Random shots like the girl out on a date, at cheer practice, shopping with her friends."

"Nate's had the girl followed." Another thought occurred to her. "Unless maybe he's pulling them from her social media sites?"

Adam shook his head. "Tami checked. She showed me a couple, they were taken with a long-range lens."

The sudden pitching of her stomach had her swallowing hard. Buzzing sounded in her ears. "He's going to do something awful to Eli if he can get to him."

"Lyssie." Hunt turned her face to his. "Griff won't let them touch him."

Not enough. "Can he take them away? Anywhere? I'll pay. Please." All she could think of was that tiny baby in her arms, how much she'd loved him in those few moments. Then the video Hunt had gotten for her, the one she'd watched a hundred times in the last few days. That beautiful little boy… She wouldn't let Nate hurt him.

Hunt considered that. "Not a bad idea, actually. I have the perfect place if the parents are willing."

She grabbed onto his arm. "Where?"

"My friend Logan Knight has a huge horse ranch in Texas. Logan still works part time for Once A Marine from there and he's good. There, with him and Griff, the kid and his parents will be untouchable. They'll have the huge ranch to move around on."

"I agree," Adam said. "You call Logan, I'll call Griff."

Before she knew it, the two men had it arranged. Mark and Janis, Eli's parents, agreed, a private plane chartered and they'd be in Texas by nightfall.

Hunt took her hand. "You okay?"

She inhaled a deep breath and faced him. "What I am is pissed." Furious heat blasted out of her skin. "Nate Madden thought he could seduce and control me, and use my son to do it? Not happening." Taking her hand away, she surged up to her feet. "I'm not the first. He's left that other poor woman living in terror and his mother dead, but I was his ultimate mark, his final prize, and I am no man's prize." God, she was just damned mad. When she'd first run to Hunt, she'd been scared and unsure. But now?

"We need to screw with Nate's plans. Show him he's not scaring me." She slapped her hand down on the back of her chair. "And swear to God, he'd better not hurt another dog." That was another thing that had sickened and enraged her, but the good news was the dog would recover and the vet had located his owners through a microchip in the animal. The dog had been stolen right out of their car when the owner ran back in the house for something. So many thoughts churned through her head. Then an idea hit her. "Let's send the ring back to Nate."

Hunt smiled. "He ordered you to wear it, and you

figuratively flip him off."

"Good start," Adam said. "Then I think you two should show up in public together, maybe this weekend, and make sure a picture turns up on social media."

"Like at an event or something? That will put Hunt in the public eye, and then this place will be swarmed with media. It'll be ugly."

"He means like a date," Hunt said. "Show Madden you've moved on. That you are so not afraid of him, you'll flaunt me in his face."

Alyssa looked down into his eyes. Remote. Cold. Angry. Determined. "A fake date. I see." It made sense. That would enrage Nate.

She nodded slowly, ignoring the distaste of using this thing between her and Hunt to bait her ex. Taking something that had been real to her—and temporary, she knew that, but still real—and make it fake. That's how she'd started with Nate, fake dates, and look how that had ended. But now wasn't the time to be weak.

"All right. A fake date. Not like I haven't done that before."

. . .

The rest of the night her words echoed in his head. Through their quiet dinner, and as Lyssie fiddled with her website, losing herself as she worked, occasionally biting on her thumbnail, Hunt hadn't been able to stop watching her. A combination of fire and sweetness that twisted him up like a pretzel. So much so it drove him out to his studio just to think.

A fake date. Not like I haven't done that before.

With Madden, that asshole who'd used her, manipulated

her then threatened her. Damn it. Hunt stretched his neck and flexed his fingers. What he was doing was no better. Oh yeah, he was protecting her and refusing to take payment.

But then he seduced her.

Christ. That look in her eyes, the absolute sadness when she'd agreed that they'd do a fake date this weekend. There was nothing fake about what he and Lyssie had. What was worse, she really hadn't dated after giving up her baby. He was pretty sure the only two men she'd been with had been Scott and Nate, neither of whom had treated her as she deserved.

This was bullshit. Oh, he understood the tactical part of pushing Nate's buttons, and frankly it appealed to him. If Hunt got really lucky, that slick bastard would try to eliminate Hunt to get him out of the way. Both Adam and Hunt were hoping for that. The prick would find himself dead or hurt badly enough to wish he was dead. So he was onboard with that. But not Lyssie believing he couldn't be bothered to take her out on a real date. To make a goddamned effort for her, spend real time with her and show her how she deserved to be treated.

His eyes caught on the piece he was working on. Not his nightmares. No, this one was special, more powerful in its own way. Lyssie. He ran his finger along the emerging piece, but the cool clay wasn't what he wanted to touch. He wanted to hold the flesh and blood woman in his house. Talk to her. Be with her. Erase the sadness from her eyes. *Enough.* After covering his work and cleaning his hands, he headed across the patio and into the house. Low music and the scent of warm chocolate greeted him. His mouth watered.

Then he caught sight of Lyssie. She had her back to him by the stove in tight white shorts, scooping brownies out of a pan directly into her mouth. With the music, she hadn't heard him come in. He forgot everything but the sexy woman in his kitchen. Seeing her like this, eating brownies and dancing, drew him to her. He moved quietly up behind her and slapped his hands down on the counter, caging her. "Whatcha doing?"

She yelped, twisting her head around. Her expression screamed *busted*. "Umm, cutting the brownies?"

"With a spoon?"

Color splashed over her cheeks. Her chin went up. "It's a more efficient system. No plates to wash."

"Were you going to eat the entire pan by yourself?"

"Maybe."

Despite his guilt, he grinned. Wrapping his hand around hers, he scooped up a spoonful of warm brownie, intending to steal a bite.

Her eyes flared. She leaned in and snatched the bite off the spoon before he could.

Hot. So hot. Forgetting his concern for a second, he said, "Bad girl." He caught her ponytail and lowered his mouth to hers. Watching her eyes widen and hearing her breath hitch did things to his chest. "That was my bite." He licked a leisurely stroke across her lips, tasting her skin and chocolate, coaxing her to open and share with him.

Her mouth parted and she slid her tongue against his. His brain melted at the taste of Lyssie and chocolate. Blood rushed, his heart pounded, and fire licked along his nerves. But he pulled back, determined to talk to her. "Are you baking brownies because you're worried about Eli?"

"No. Griff texted me that they are at the Knight Ranch, and everything's good."

Excellent. Hunt had given Griff her number and now it was time Hunt manned up. "All right, then we need to talk about the date."

"Okay." She put the spoon down and faced him.

"I don't want a fake date with you."

The heat in her eyes died. Twisting away, she grabbed a sponge and started cleaning up. "Fine. Next week I'll go to Maxine's party. It's a week from Friday. I assume you and the others can provide protection? It's at Jinx Restaurant in Malibu, and Nate knows I'm going. Maybe he'll try something there. In fact, I'll have Maxine mention on her social media sites that I'm hosting the party, and that will—"

"Lyssie."

For one second, she stood with her back to him, her head angled down, that sponge in her hand. Then she squared her shoulders and pivoted. "What?"

After taking the sponge from her hand, he tossed it and laid his palms on her hips. "We'll go to Maxine's party." He understood how much her friend meant to her, and they'd go.

"Thanks."

"I'd like very much to take you on a date, a real one. I'll have Erin get a couple pics and post them to bait Madden, then you're all mine."

"You want to go on a real date?"

"Very much." He wanted to do something no one else did for her, which meant it had to be damned special. Anyone could take her to expensive dinners, but Hunt had to figure out something that would rock her world, while keeping her safe, of course. "So how about it, princess? Will you go on a date with me?"

Chapter Eleven

Alyssa stood at the side of the four-person basket as they sailed nearly two thousand feet off the ground. Above them, duel burners fired hot air into the brightly colored balloon. Aside from the sounds of the burners, it was quiet up here. So serene it felt like she could almost touch heaven. With her camera, she captured a blanket of fog nestled between the mountains.

"So tell me, princess, are you impressed with our date?" Hunt spoke into her ear.

Shivers cascaded over her skin. His voice could do that to her. He stood close behind her, one arm on the basket, the other on her hip, holding her steady so she could film. For three days he'd refused to tell her where he was taking her for their date, only that she had to be ready before daybreak early Saturday morning.

It hadn't been until they pulled up to the launch site and she saw the balloon rising off the ground as the burners inflated it that she'd gotten her answer. "It's perfect." Erin had met them there and gotten a few shots of them posing in front of the balloon and in the basket before takeoff.

Now they were on their *real date*. She lowered her camera, then reached down and tucked it into her bag.

"Done filming?"

Alyssa laid her hand over his on her hip. "I want to experience this, feel it." The beauty floated by. They were moving pretty fast, but it felt as if they were lazily drifting, just the two of them and their pilot. "How did you think of this?"

Hunt angled his face over her shoulder to look down at her. "I wanted to do something you'd remember. I booked a private ride with someone I trust. Your safety comes first and Mac is discreet."

Her heart tripped. He'd taken a lot of safety precautions including making sure they left in the dark so Lyssie wouldn't be spotted. He'd gone to a lot of trouble to give her special moments. "I won't forget." Not this balloon ride, and not him.

Lowering his mouth to her ear, he said, "Don't look at me like that. We're not alone."

"And if we were?" Their pilot, Mac, was on the other side of the basket, controlling the burners and giving them space.

Hunt made a noise in his chest. Burying his mouth against her ear, he pitched his voice into a husky whisper. "We're going to be alone in part two of our date. I'll show you then exactly what I plan to do to you."

Anticipation shivered through her, while warmth flooded her chest. Hunt was giving her special memories and stealing her heart.

• • •

The croissant melted in Alyssa's mouth. She sat on the floor, resting her back against the couch of the secluded cabin Hunt had secured from a friend. Between them was a plate mounded with warm croissants, cheese, and fresh melons. A fire crackled in the corner fireplace, music played softly in the background.

"So this is part two, the romantic getaway." She'd read that on Erin's Facebook page with a picture of the two of them taking off in the hot air balloon. Then Maxine had shared it as per the plan. She reached for her phone to check—

Hunt slipped her cell from her hand and tossed it aside. "This is our weekend, Lyssie. Forget the posts. Sienna is monitoring everything, and Adam is at my house. We put up more cameras to watch who tries to get access. If Madden shows up, we'll capture him on video. Plus Cooper is watching him. This is our time now." He picked up a strawberry, dipped it in fresh whipped cream and fed it to her.

Damn that was good.

"Talk to me, tell me how your website is going."

Startled, she lifted her eyes. "Really?"

A smile broke out on his face, and he poured her some more coffee. "I love listening to you talk about Streets of Valor. You glow with passion and care so much. So yeah." Handing her the cup, he said, "Really. I want to know."

Hot pleasure danced in her stomach and in seconds she spilled out all her dreams. How much she loved doing it, loved meeting these people who lived through harsh realities and found a way to survive and triumph. Before she knew it, they'd polished off the food, Mimosas and coffee. "Anyway, the site is essentially ready when I want to launch it. But not now, I don't want the soap opera of my life to distract from the stories and people I want to showcase."

"Makes sense." Hunt played with a strand of her hair, his eyes glinting. "The videos and pictures you showed me are incredible, powerful."

"You wormed those out of me after giving me that statue."

"Yeah, I guess I did. Maybe I owe you for that."

His intense stare combined with the gentle touch as he played with her hair kicked up the low-grade sizzle that always hummed between them. "You'll show me another of your sculptures?" Hope swelled in her. Alyssa wanted to understand what tortured him, what woke him in the nights and drove him out to the studio. She'd woken in his bed alone and worried, but unable to help him.

He didn't respond for a few seconds.

Alyssa held her breath. What was he thinking?

"Yes." Taking his hand from her hair, he fluidly rose to his feet. "But this one is special, Lyssie. It's not death."

Her mouth dried. "No?"

"It's you."

"You sculpted me?" What did that mean? She rolled to sit on her knees. "Now? You brought it here?"

He nodded. "You can film it if you want, Lyssie. If you hate it or it embarrasses you, I'll make sure no one else ever sees it, but it's mine. Understood?"

That possession in his voice flooded her. "Yes."

He turned and strode out.

She scrambled to get her camera, mostly to calm her spinning thoughts.

He came in with it wrapped in a towel. Excitement and nerves clattered in her veins. Why did this mean so much to her? To get control, she trained her camera on Hunt. He stopped at the table behind the couch. "This is how I see you. My beautiful Lyssie." Hunt unwrapped the statue and put it on the tall table.

She forgot about videoing and set her camera aside. The statue was a woman on her knees, arching back, arms reaching out and hair sweeping down. The lines were fluid and sensual arcs. Her long neck curved into her shoulders and breasts. Her knees were slightly parted, her sex hinted at but not defined. But the most stunning part, the part that caused a rushing sensation in Alyssa's head, was that a circular section of the woman's belly was missing. And there, floating in that space, was a ruby dragon tear, similar to the one she had inked on her stomach.

Moving closer, she drew her finger down one smooth arm, along the ribs to the hips. She touched cool dried clay yet she saw a warm-blooded, sensual and emotional woman.

Sexual. Vulnerable. Strong. Weak. Lover. And that tear-drop—a mother.

He'd captured her, yet with more beauty than she could ever have imagined.

"Say something."

His voice was right behind her. She turned, staring up into his eyes. "That's how you see me?"

"Yes."

"She's magnificent." Hunt had always been talented, but this was extraordinary. "What's she reaching for?"

"Her dreams."

He'd heard her, understood that she needed to follow her passion. "I don't see myself as that sexual."

"I do." Hunt tucked his hand beneath her hair, sliding his thumb along the sensitive line of her throat. "Does it embarrass you that it's a nude?"

Her nipples pebbled at his touch, but it was his gaze that pulled out her truth. "It's a little overwhelming, but it's also sexy that your hands did that while thinking of me."

Lowering his head until his eyes burned into hers, Hunt said softly, "Lyssie."

His scent surrounded her. "What?"

"We're in part two. This date is ours, just you and me, and I want to make love to you." He tugged her face closer and covered her mouth with his, sliding his tongue in, taking possession.

Her skin sizzled with the simmering need that he'd ignited on the balloon ride. When Hunt's fingers dropped to the hem of her shirt, she pulled back and raised her arms for him to tug it off.

Hunt fingered the lace edge of her sheer, low-cut pink bra. "You've been wearing this beneath your clothes all day?"

Emboldened, wanting to be the woman he sculpted, she undid her jeans and shimmied them down, revealing her barely-there lace panties. "I wanted to surprise you." It occurred to her that she hadn't really dressed up for him or made any big effort. With Hunt, she never felt like she had to. But she wanted to.

He fished a condom out of his pocket and tossed it down on the table. In seconds, he stripped off his shoes, pants, shirt, boxers, until all he wore was the ink and a straining erection.

She traced the lines of the script and tribal markings over his shoulders and biceps, mapping every bulge and dip. Rising on her toes, she buried her nose in his throat, inhaling the scent of Hunt. Finding his pulse, she lapped at it.

Hunt drew his fingers down the line of her bra, then unhooked the front clasp and parted the lacy material. Pushing it off her shoulders, he brushed his knuckles along the sensitive undersides. Her nipples tightened, the peaks going rigid. "That's hot." He leaned down and sucked. Hard. Just how she liked it. Needed it. She threaded her fingers in his hair as he laved attention on one then the other. Desperate to touch him, she skated her hands over his rippled muscles to grip his hard length. She loved the feel of his cock, long and thick, heated steel beneath her stroking fingers.

He lifted his head. "More, Lyssie. I need to taste you."

Before she could answer, or think, he dropped to his knees and peeled off her panties. His large hands, both deadly and talented, spread her open.

The cool air hit her sensitized folds, followed by his warm breath. Her nerves lit up. He pressed his huge ink-covered shoulders in between her thighs and dragged his tongue along her cleft.

Her belly clamped and hot need pooled. She shot her hand out, grabbing the table. The cool wood was a stark contrast to his warm, slightly rough tongue.

"So damned good." Hunt growled the words and buried his face in her, licking and sucking until her legs shook.

It was building too fast, the pleasure coming at her. The intensity almost frightened her. "Hunt." She dug her fingers into his shoulders. Couldn't control it. "I'll fall."

He sat back, his eyes dilated, mouth wet. "Never. With me you'll fly, not fall." He snapped upright, ripped open the condom, and rolled it over his length. His chest rose and fell in harsh breaths, his cock bouncing in eagerness.

Moving behind her, he tugged her back to his front, his erection branding her lower back. "I'm going to hold you, Lyssie. You won't fall." Pushing her hair aside, he kissed along the curve of her neck, sending streaks to her nipples. Her clit swelled and throbbed.

Safe. Sexy. Cared for. It all filled her, ramping up her need. With no fear, she just felt.

Hunt licked her ear. "I've never wanted anyone like I want you. Need you. I can't let you go."

She turned her head. His gorgeous eyes churned with lust, and something thicker. "Don't let go."

"I need you like this, to possess you." Taking her hands, he bent her over, placing her palms on the table. He dragged his knuckles down her spine, gripped her hips to press the head of his erection in, paused, and then thrust, full and deep, filling and owning her. Touching all the places no one else could.

He covered her back, one hand slapping down next to hers, the other wrapped around her waist. "Mine, Lyssie."

Two words undid them both. He thrust, pounded, hammered into her, driving her so high she couldn't bear it.

Hunt panted into her ear, "Look at the statue. That's what I feel and see when I'm inside you."

Alyssa took in the beauty Hunt created with his hands. She stared until he took her over the edge, then wild pleasure blinded her to everything but Hunt.

Alyssa flew in the arms of the man she was falling in

love with.

• • •

Wearing just his boxers, Hunt reclined on one side of the couch with Lyssie's feet in his lap. Every time he pressed his thumb into her arch, she moaned. He'd found another spot that made his girl hot. He loved discovering new details.

She leaned against the opposite side, filming the statue. "Hold it for me."

Wrapping his hand around the statue, he eyed her in her bra and panties. "How about we trade? You hold the statue and I'll video you." Her hair was tousled, her skin still flushed and her eyes...damn.

"Nope. I don't do underwear shots. Sorry. And believe me, I've had offers, including from *Playboy Magazine*."

Hunt fumbled the statue, the image of Lyssie spread out, nude and posing...other men seeing her. "Oh hell no." Curling his hand around her slender foot, he leaned forward. "I don't share, cover girl."

She lowered the camera. "How is it different? You've sculpted me nude. Would you show that?"

Hunt shifted his gaze to the sculpture. A part of him wanted to. Sharing the awakening beauty of Lyssie, the way she rose and stretched was more than sensual. It was a woman embracing her pain and power. Would he show it? He returned his attention to her. "I don't feel the need to lock it up in the dark like I do my other work."

Picking up her camera, she asked, "Why, Hunt? Why do you lock your studio, keep everyone out?"

He set the statue down and leaned back. "Interviewing

me?"

"You sculpted me nude and you're keeping it. I'm trusting you not to show that until I'm ready."

"Point?"

"You revealed me right down to the dragon tear that is my way of carrying Eli with me. People saw the tat if I was in a swimsuit, but only you know the true significance of it and you put it in that statue. I trust you." Moving her camera, she pinned her gaze on him. "I love that statue, love seeing me through your eyes. Let me do that for you. Talk to me. I have a lot of footage of you that I want to create into the story of you through my eyes. I want to give you that. No one else, just you." She smiled and added, "Well, us, because like that statue of me is yours, I'm keeping a copy of this for me. A memory of us."

He didn't have it in him to resist her. Didn't want to. Lyssie's gentle fierceness melted the layers of ice in him until she made him burn and feel. Yeah, she trusted him with that statue, but it went deeper, like that moment when he'd been on his knees tasting her, savoring her, unable to get enough and she'd called to him. She'd been flying too high with nothing to hold on to, afraid she'd fall.

She called to him. Needed him. Trusted him to help her.

He'd gone nearly feral in that second. Taking her hard, driving her higher while keeping her safe in his arms. He'd never let her fall. So this right now? He wanted to do it, to give her that same trust. Who was the man Lyssie saw through her camera? The one she trusted so implicitly in her most vulnerable moment?

She asked why he locked his studio. Slowly, he gathered his thoughts. "I go into my studio to vent." He wrapped his hands around her feet in his lap, the connection keeping him settled. "As a sniper, I'd shut down to do the job, became cold and emotionless. When I came home, I remained disconnected. But after that mall shooting, seeing the way Rachel looked at me, it cracked the tight control I had on my emotions. I started having nightmares, reliving missions. Only, in my nightmares, I wasn't cold and in absolute control like I had been in real life. Instead, I felt it all—fear, remorse, hatred and sickness at seeing a man die from my bullet. Even after I woke in a cold sweat, I couldn't stop it unless I sculpted. Once I had the nightmare vented into clay, I put it on the shelf and locked it in that room."

She put down her camera, pulled her feet back.

For one second, Hunt thought she was going to run away from him, tell him to never touch her again. Vast emptiness swelled in his chest. Had he told her too much? Finally made her understand what he was?

Lyssie went up on her knees and flung herself at him.

Pure reflex kicked in and Hunt caught her, pulling her up to his chest. Damn, what just happened? Her warm skin pressed against his, vanilla and sunshine fragrance filled his chest where a second ago it'd been a desert of fear and emptiness. She had her head tucked beneath his chin, her silky hair spread out on his shoulder and neck. He shifted, sliding down to hold her against him, and stroked her hair. "What's this, baby? Are you upset?"

She laid her palm over his bullet tat. "No. I just want to hold you."

Her breath rippled across his skin, creating fissions of emotions sliding into him. "Not that I'm complaining, but why?"

She lifted her head. "Because I care about you. You've spent most of your adult life protecting others. Even now you're protecting your family from seeing the part of you that you think will hurt them."

She saw that? "It would hurt them. My parents dedicated their lives to promoting peace over violence. They protested wars, while raising money to help veterans. If they see what I've become, they'll look at me differently."

"Like Rachel?"

"Yes, but I didn't have any attachment to Rachel. I tried, but it wasn't there." Which hadn't been fair to her. In hindsight, he realized he really was a cold bastard. Using her to try and figure out how to be normal again. At least he was being honest with Lyssie.

"Hunt, they love you."

"I know and that's why it would hurt them too much." He dragged his hand down to settle on the curve of her back. "And there are some things no one can ever know."

• • •

Alyssa pushed up to straddle his stomach so she could see him better. "What things? Like top secret, you'd have to kill me if you told me things?"

Hunt's light blue eyes frosted. "Don't even joke about that, Alyssa."

Hearing her full name from him jarred her. "I… Sorry." His chest expanded and he slowly exhaled. She stared at that bullet inked over his heart, trying to understand what she'd said wrong.

Hunt took her hands in his, threading their fingers.

"Joking about me killing you is…" He pulled his mouth into a tight line, but his fingers around hers were gentle. "It's too close to a really sore spot with me."

The sudden agony swimming in his eyes tugged on her heart and made her eyes burn. Look at all he'd done for her, taking her on this date, letting her film him, sharing parts of himself, and she tossed off some thoughtless comment. "I'll be more careful."

He closed his eyes, and when he opened them, the pain was gone. "I don't want you to be careful. This, what we have, it's honest. Neither of us is pretending to be something we're not." He rubbed his thumbs over her hands. "My response was honest."

She could lose herself in his eyes and touch. The way he held her hands with such intimacy and trust fed into her. Little by little, he gave her these pieces of himself, trusting her with them. Her mouth dried. "Does it ever feel like we're maybe getting too intense? Too fast?"

"From the second you walked into Once A Marine."

"Is this how most short-term hookups are?"

"No." He leaned up, his mouth brushing hers, then his eyes commanded her gaze. "You're not a hookup. You're my lover, and right now, you are making me want more. Crave more. I want to go to bed with you, get up with you, take you on dates, make you dinner while you tell me about your day working on your Streets of Valor website. I want to sculpt every wicked image of you I can come up with, and believe me, I can come up with a lot. You are not a hookup to me, baby girl."

A blast of hot want gushed up from her soul to feed her foolish hopes. "You want more? Like keep seeing each other after this job is over more?"

Long beats passed as he ground his jaw. He glanced over at the statue on the table behind the couch. "That's the first time in years I could sculpt something besides my nightmares." Swinging his attention to hers, he squeezed her hands in his. "You make me want to be normal and build a real relationship with you, but that switch is there."

This, the way he talked to her and told her his struggles wrapped around her chest. She wanted to understand. "Your sniper switch? Are you really so afraid of that? I wasn't upset at the cliffs. I'll never be mad at you for trying to protect me." How could she be? Hunt had always made her feel safe. He'd changed, there was no doubt about that. The all-American boy had come back a hard man, but he didn't scare her.

Haunted shadows lurked in his eyes. "What really scares me is that one day I could flip that switch and not be able to turn it off."

It took long seconds for the meaning to sink in. Hunt feared he'd lose control of the killer inside him. "No." She shook her head so hard her hair whipped around her. "You're not a killer. Not like that."

It couldn't happen.

Could it?

Chapter Twelve

Wednesday afternoon, Alyssa ignored another pleading text from her stepfather. *You're not only ruining your life, but mine, Nate's and everyone's at Dragon Wing. How can you do this to your mother's company? Shacking up with some bodyguard and...*

Delete. She had to do it before she gave in to the temptation to try to explain to Parker that Nate had threatened her and her son that she'd never told Parker about. Had Nate told him about Eli? No, she decided as she worked through the emails and various things Maxine had forwarded to her. Nate had hoarded that info to use against her.

Lifting her head, she glanced out to Hunt. He sat at the wrought iron table, breaking down and cleaning his two weapons. His hands moved with sure precision, his focus sharp. He had on shorts and another T-shirt that showcased his powerful shoulders.

They'd returned from the cabin Sunday, the street

clogged with news media and both of them tense as hell, but nothing happened. They'd reviewed the camera footage, no Nate. He hadn't called, hadn't texted, not after getting her ring back or seeing the picture of her and Hunt on their date. Media trailed him, catching sight of him looking grim. One reporter managed to ask him how he was holding up.

He'd looked right into the camera. "Alyssa is my life. I can't believe this is happening. Her mother would be devastated." Then he'd shaken his head and walked into the building.

He was being painted as the victim while social media called her names and told Hunt to run while he could. Dump her cheating ass. Their plan hadn't done anything but make the world hate Alyssa Brooks more. She took a breath. Didn't matter. She'd been hated before when her mom died.

Hunt finished cleaning and swiftly reassembled the gun, then he lifted his head, his gaze catching hers through the screen of the sliding glass door separating them.

The impact flipped her stomach. *You're my lover. And right now, you are making me want more. Crave more.* God, she did too, but was it possible? Looking into his eyes, she desperately wanted a future with him.

His mouth curved, and her earlier tension softened. In that moment, she saw both the artistic boy she remembered and the hardened man she was falling for. She smiled back. Her phone dinged, shattering the moment. Glancing at the text from another unknown number, she gasped. The thumbnail picture showed a face she recognized.

Maxine. Her assistant. Crap. Tapping it opened the picture full screen. "Oh God." A large cop had Maxine thrown face down on the hood of her yellow Mustang, her hands cuffed behind her back. And her face? Shock and fear.

Maxine was never afraid. Never. Rage punched her. The text accompanying the picture read, *Apparently your administrative assistant that I told you to fire repeatedly is a thief.*

Nate, that asswipe. Maxine was not a thief. Blinding fury exploded with a force that consumed her. Jabbing at her phone, she pulled up her contacts and called the scumsucking bastard.

"Now I have your attention."

His voice jacked her rage to nuclear. "What did you do? Maxine's not a thief!"

A hand came down on her arm. She jerked her head up to see Hunt staring at her, his face hard. "Madden?" he mouthed.

She nodded, her chest tight at the thought of Maxine in handcuffs. In jail.

Hunt leaned his head close to hear.

"She stole from me," Nate said in her ear. "My Rolex and laptop were found in her car."

It took a couple heartbeats for her to fully grasp it. "You set her up."

"I'm done fucking with you, Alyssa. You'll get your ass back here and do every damned thing I tell you to and I'll drop the charges against her."

"And if I don't?"

"I'll make sure Maxine ends up in prison, gets her own personal shower scene and bleeds out."

The image splashed violently across her mind and she had to slap her hand over her mouth as nausea shot up her throat.

Hunt grabbed the phone, hung it up, and dropped down

to his haunches. "Look at me and breathe. I heard some of that but I need to know all of it."

Don't vomit. Think. Alyssa took her phone back and pulled up the text message, then showed Hunt.

"That fucker."

"He set her up. Maxine's not a thief." She grabbed his arm, digging her fingers into the unyielding muscles.

He nodded. "Is she in Malibu?"

"Yes."

Hunt grabbed his phone, thumbed the screen. "Hang on."

"Hunt, what do you need?" Sienna's voice came through the speaker.

"We have a situation. Madden made his move. Maxine Lord was arrested. It looks like outside a…" He looked up at her.

Alyssa studied the picture, forcing herself to look past Maxine thrown over the hood of the car and cuffed. "Bank in Malibu." She named it for him.

Hunt nodded and repeated the information. "Get a lawyer over to the Malibu station and get her released. Nothing showed in her background check, so she doesn't have a record. Use Alyssa's name, pull in favors, whatever it takes. Just get her out."

As soon as he ended the call, he pulled her into his arms. "She's going to be okay, Lyssie. We're leaving in the morning as planned, and you'll see her soon." He rubbed her back, then looked down into her face. "Do you know her family?"

"She has a mom and brother. Jeff went to college with us."

"Call them so they can be at the station with her when

they release her. She won't be alone tonight."

Her eyes burned with grateful tears. Hunt hadn't met Maxine, but he knew Alyssa cared so he thought of things like making sure she wasn't alone when she got out of jail.

• • •

Thursday evening, Hunt dropped their bags and looked around Lyssie's house in Malibu. After leaving the vineyard, they'd driven straight to Maxine's brother's house and had dinner there. It'd been a long day and he was glad to have Lyssie where he knew she was safe. Cooper had made sure the house was secure.

He'd been here once before while she packed to go to Sonoma. That time he'd checked the main floor then stayed in the living room and made some calls while she gathered her things. Now he took a closer look around. The house was built on the cliffs overlooking the Pacific Ocean. White walls and marble floors led straight through an elegantly appointed living room to a dining room with a natural cut table to the focal point of the entire living space—the wall of sliding glass panels. Beyond that was a deck built out on stilts and a spectacular ocean view. He loved the view, but the house was cold. Even the gourmet kitchen was all show and little heart. "Looks like a magazine." The only real personal touch was a painting done by his mother over her fireplace.

"Professionally decorated, and Jessie my housekeeper keeps it perfect." She waved her hand. "Let's put our stuff in the bedroom, then I have something to show you."

Hunt followed her down a hallway on the right. They passed a hall bathroom and guest bedroom, then went into the master. The massive bed faced a set of French doors with a view of the cliffs and ocean. He liked it a lot as long as he didn't think of another man in her bed, touching her.

He locked his jaw at the memory of her telling him that her ex liked her camera-ready, makeup and hair done, wearing tasteful lingerie. All she had to wear for him was the desire for his touch.

"My new bed came." She ran her hand over the snowy white comforter then touched the piles of pale blue and gray pillows. "It's perfect, better than the picture. I love it."

It took him a second to mentally catch up. "You ordered a new bed? You weren't even here."

"My housekeeper took care of the delivery, washing the new linens, and making the bed."

Watching the way she dragged her fingers over the soft plush comforter, his blood heated. He moved up and wrapped his arms around her. Lyssie felt damn good against his body, her vanilla and sunshine scent filling his lungs. "Want to break in your new bed?" He wanted her, hell, he always wanted her, but it'd been a long day. "If you're too tired for sex, we could watch a movie until you fall asleep." She always curled up on him like a kitten and dropped off to sleep.

She turned in his arms and kissed him, stealing his breath and hardening his cock. "There's something I want to show you." She grabbed his hand then paused, a gleam filling her brown eyes. "We could bring a condom."

That piqued his interest. The strain that had lurked in her face all night had drained once they'd gotten to Maxine's and seen that she appeared fine aside from the fiery rage at Madden. Now sparks of sexy mischievousness and a little shyness or nerves brightened Lyssie's eyes. Shoving a condom in his pocket, he asked, "You seducing me?"

She grabbed his hand. "Come find out."

They crossed the living space and kitchen into another hallway ending in a flight of stairs going down. Quirky and cool. The stairs led to a sunlit rec room. This wing of the house was past the garage and on the lower slope end of the cliff, giving her a bottom level. No sign of a professional decorator here. She'd painted the walls a soft orange that reminded him of that last ray of light as the sun set over the ocean. There was a tanned leather couch facing a huge flat screen TV. Behind that was a ping-pong table. Across the room was a sliding door with a tiny deck big enough for a couple chairs, with a sturdy metal railing and a sheer drop-off down to the beach and ocean. Beautiful and possibly treacherous. Lyssie really didn't have a fear of heights.

Butting up against the staircase wall was a curved wet bar with stools. It was the wall behind that grabbed his full attention. Dozens of photos were grouped artfully. Many were of kids and some adults with physical issues but all wearing smiles. Several had companion dogs.

This room was the real Lyssie. Studying the pictures, one caught his interest. "That's your parents." He didn't recall ever meeting her dad before he died, but he'd seen photos. This one was against a bright blue sky surrounded by... "Castle ruins?"

"That's where my dad asked my mom to marry him in Scotland, away from all the Hollywood mania that surrounded my mom at the time. They looked so happy there."

Oh, now he understood her reason for wanting to go to Scotland. She had more pictures, a lot of him and his family.

"There are two empty spaces."

"Nate. I took them down the night I gave his ring back. If I entertain for work it's upstairs, but this room is mine and I don't want him in here. Besides, he thought this room was tacky, and wanted me to redo it in a theater room."

Hunt would be perfectly happy on that couch with a beer watching an action flick or his beloved UFC. "You don't like your upstairs?"

A grimace crossed her face. "I like the deck and my bedroom, the rest is boring, generic."

"Honey, I'm not sure you're doing this heiress thing right. You have the money to make your house however you want it."

"I did. I have this room and put in an elevator."

"Where's the elevator?"

"Hidden panel in the hallway to the stairs."

Why would she...? His gaze went to the pictures. "For your friends?" A few of them were in wheelchairs.

"Sometimes we have little get-togethers here. Play some ping-pong or watch TV." She tugged his hand. "I have something else to show you." She took him by a small office, a bathroom, then into the last room.

The first thing he saw was the spinning table used for sculpting. There was also a sturdy worktable piled with bags, a stool, a cabinet and in the corner a comfortable looking club chair.

"I thought you could use this for your studio while we're here. This door handle locks. When Cooper put the new locks in, I had him do a separate one for this room. I'll give you the key. No one will come in here. You can arrange it how you like. If you need more stuff, we'll get it."

For a few seconds, he just stood there, her words pouring over his back while he tried to make sense of the room. *A studio. To sculpt.* Finally her silence got his attention. Settling his hands on her shoulders, he blurted out, "You did this? When?"

"After you told me how important your studio is at the cabin. I consulted with Erin and ordered everything and had it delivered. Jessie, my housekeeper, put it all in here." She bit her lip, swaying nervously. "For however long we're here, I wanted you to have this in case you have nightmares and need to sculpt, or if you just want to. You have your own space."

Lyssie had heard him and cared enough to do this. It boggled his mind.

"You don't have to use it. It was just a thought. Not a big deal."

It was a big fucking deal, so big it tightened his throat. She understood his need to sculpt. He tugged her into his arms. "I love it, thank you, Lyssie. It's perfect."

Her smile lit up his insides. "Good. You can organize this later. I'll help if you want." She tugged him out of the room, closed the door, locked it and handed him the key. "It's yours." Without another word she started back to the rec room.

That small silver key in his hand felt more significant than just a key to a door. A gift from a woman who gave him the space he needed. Tucking it into his pocket, he latched onto her hand.

Hunt eyed the ping-pong table. "I'd forgotten your obsession with ping-pong."

Her grin curved wickedly. "That's why I had you bring

the condom down here. Want to play? If you win, you get what you want, and if I win, I get what I want."

Oh, he was very interested, even more as he understood that this was the part of Lyssie's house she loved and she was sharing it with him in a special way. He curled his arm around her waist. "What do you want, princess? Be specific. If we're betting, I want to know what I'm risking here. If I win, I get to peel off your clothes, and bend you over the ping-pong table."

Her breath hitched but she lifted her chin. "If I win, you have to strip for me and let me kiss you anywhere I want as long as I want."

He sucked in a breath, his body humming with need that shot straight to his groin. The image of her on her knees, her silky hair sliding along his thighs… "Get the paddles." He barely got the words out.

After four games, they were tied. Lyssie glared at him. "How can you be this good?"

He laughed at her disgruntlement. "Sniper skills, baby. Fast reflexes, superior hand–eye coordination, and the ability to judge distance and wind conditions to hit any target." He tossed her the ball. "Your serve. Game five is the tiebreaker. Bring it."

She caught the ball then set it and the paddle down. "I call unfair advantage. I need to even things up."

"That right? What are you going to do, tie one hand behind my back? I'll still win." The words dried up as Lyssie whipped off her T-shirt. Backlit by the sun streaming through the window, her brown hair gleamed as it fell around her bare shoulders. Hunt slowly trailed his gaze down her long throat to her breasts tipped with dark nipples that stiffened into peaks before his eyes.

His mouth dried.

He continued his inspection over her rib cage then down her flat belly to the delicate tattoo peeking over her jeans riding low on her hip bones. His hands itched to mold and shape her alluring lines, while sucking on her—

Hell. Shifting his hips to accommodate his hardening cock, he forced himself to look up. "That's cheating."

She flashed him a kick-ass grin. "What? The big bad sniper is distracted by this?" She skated her fingers up her belly and circled the small mounds of her breasts.

"I won't be distracted when I have you bent over this table and use this paddle on your ass. Serve."

• • •

Alyssa never bounced so much in her life, but it worked. She had two points on Hunt. "Game point, Marine. Ready to admit defeat?"

"Are you gloating?"

She laughed, her entire body humming with happiness. Feeling lighter and braver than she had in years, Alyssa said, "It's not gloating when you've got game." She tossed up the ball and served.

Hunt jerked his gaze from her breasts and returned the serve a fraction too late. It flew over the side of the table.

"I win!" Alyssa threw up her hands and shimmied. "You lose."

"Keep on dancing, princess. It's hot."

"I win, you have to do what I say. You can't welch."

Hunt twisted the paddle in his hand, a sexy glint in his

eyes. "I never welch. But we have a problem, sweetheart." His voice lowered into a silky command and he advanced on her slowly, with sizzling intent glowing in his eyes.

Danger and excitement skittered and popped. "What?"

He stopped two feet from her, between the ping-pong table and the back of the sofa. "You cheated to get your win. Hold this." He held out his hand.

She dropped her gaze to the paddle. Why didn't he just set it down? She wrapped her fingers around the handle and reached to put it on the table.

"No. Hold it." Hunt snapped the order while digging his hand into his pocket and pulling out a wrapped condom. "And keep this in your other hand."

She took the condom. "Why am I holding these?"

"Cheaters don't get to ask questions." He curved his large hands around her breasts and teased her nipples. "Especially cheaters with pretty little tits that distract the hell out of me. Caused me to lose a very important match."

Every nerve homed in on his hands teasing her nipples. Hot streaks of fire shot down to her core. She clenched her thighs and arched her back. Wait, she won, not him. "So you're not going to give me my prize?"

"Oh, I'm paying up, but you have a penalty coming for cheating. You will hold onto that paddle and condom, clear?" He stripped off his shirt and pulled off his shoes and socks. Then he stood, undid his pants and stripped them off with his boxers.

Six feet plus of gloriously naked Hunt stood in her rec room. All hers for the moment. Before she could take it all in, he wrapped his arms around her shoulders and tugged her against his chest, his hot skin crushing her breasts. Gathering her hair in his hand, he tilted her head back and kissed her.

She shuddered as he invaded her mouth, his tongue hot and aggressive. A harsh ache throbbed deep inside her. Time to get a little control back. Leaving his mouth, she kissed over his jaw, down the column of his throat, vividly conscious of the paddle in her fingers and his hand wrapped around her hair, each slight tug heightening her excitement.

Going to the bullet inked over his heart and kissing it, she then dragged her tongue over his nipple. She loved the taste of him, clean with a slight salty tang. His cock jerked against her stomach. Leaning back, she looked at his erection. The thick head darkened in color and beaded with clear fluid.

Her stomach tightened. Impatience dropped her to her knees. Raising her hands, she frowned, remembering the paddle and condom she clutched. The drop of fluid swelled, his cock bouncing. Alyssa glanced up.

Hunt stared down. Wrapping his hand around his dick, he said, "Lick me. Suck."

The guttural demand stripped her down to basic need to please this man, make him burn with the same fire licking between her thighs, soaking her panties. She leaned in and dragged her tongue over his cockhead, wrenching a groan from him. Then she opened her mouth over him. The feel of his thick member sliding over her tongue and against the roof of her mouth made her moan. At the same time, she dragged the edge of the paddle up the inside of Hunt's thigh, guiding with her other hand. Once she reached his heavy ball sack, she first teased him with her knuckles, then followed that with the sponged side of the paddle, all while sucking him.

"Lyssie." Hunt dug his fingers into her scalp, thrusting in

and out of her mouth. "Jesus." After a couple more pumps, he pulled out. "Enough."

She sat back and frowned.

"Give me the paddle." He held out his hand. "Then put the condom on me."

Her stomach flipped. His cock bobbed in front of her face, his chest gleamed with a fine sheen of sweat and his eyes deepened to flame blue.

Did she trust him? Easy answer—she did right down to her heart, so she handed him the paddle. She ripped open the condom and slid it over the rigid length of his straining erection. She'd barely secured it before Hunt pulled her up on her feet.

"Undo your jeans, push them and your panties to your knees."

Her heart slammed against her ribs. She ripped open her pants and shoved them and her panties to her knees.

Hunt's gaze followed, his jaw clenching as he slid his hand between her thighs. "You're drenched." His fingers eased around her clit, circling, then glided to her entrance. A second later, he took his hand away, leaving her wanting. Before she could complain, he tugged her against him and kissed her hard, then helped her to the table. Getting behind her, he dragged the paddle over her nipples while kissing a searing wet line down the curve from her neck to her shoulder.

Alyssa tilted her head, moaning at the sensations of his damp mouth and the titillating paddle. His hard dick branded her back as he pressed against her. Working his way back to her ear, he said, "How many points did you beat me by from cheating?"

Her entire body was on fire, her skin sensitized. He scraped the paddle over her belly. Turned it sideways and slid it between her thighs. She shuddered and writhed. With Hunt there were no rules, just this clean, freeing trust. "Uh, three?"

"That's right." He licked the delicate shell of her ear. "Bend over the table, Lyssie." He moved the paddle and guided her down until the cool surface pressed against her stomach, breasts and cheek. "Three swats for three points." He moved her hair to the side and dragged the paddle down her spine.

She fisted her hands, shocked at the heat streaking through her.

"So goddamned beautiful." He scraped the sponge part over her ass while his fingers slid deep inside her.

Wet sounds filled the room as he pumped into her most intimate place. "Oh…"

The paddle came down on her ass with a soft thud. Barely more than a tap, but it reverberated through her, amplifying the feel of his fingers inside her.

Another light smack and she cried out, pushing back for more. He pressed in and out, but it wasn't enough. Desperation climbed in her.

A third gentle swap and her back arched. "Hunt." She clawed the table, swamped by frenzied desire twisting through her. Sweat coated her body and her vision grayed. Spots danced. Everything tightened impossibly…

Hunt leaned over her, kissing her shoulder. "Let go, baby. Come."

His gentle command ignited her orgasm. Everything unraveled in wild pleasure and sensation. She barely felt herself being picked up and moved.

• • •

She was so fucking gorgeous, but what sucked the breath from Hunt's lungs was Lyssie's pure surrender. *To him*, the man who'd killed so many, whose very name scared the piss out of brutal terrorists. Yet she trusted him so completely that when he lifted her, she wrapped her arms around his neck. The scent of her nearly dropped him to his knees. He battled the driving urge to put her on the ground, spread her thighs, and fuck her.

Lyssie was more than that to him, so much more. She'd just surrendered to him like no one else. His throat ached as he looked down at her flushed face. After laying her on the couch, he stripped off her shoes and pants, leaving her naked as he knelt between her legs. Her thighs fell open, revealing her swollen slick folds.

Christ. He wasn't going to be able to control himself. His cock ached, his balls squeezed. She did this to him, ripped away years of rigid control.

"Hunt, come here." She held out both her hands.

Undone by her, he gathered her hands in his, raised them over her head, and thrust into her body. "I can't hold back, Lyssie. I want to be gentle." Her walls closed around his cock, making his back burn with the need to slam into her.

She kissed his shoulder, then said, "This, Hunt. This is what I want. You…" She met his slow thrust, her fingers clenching around his. "Real. With you I'm not a prissy-ass cover girl."

"And I'm not a monster."

"Never. You're the man who never holds back who he is with me. That's what I want."

Every nerve lit on fire. Keeping hold of her hands, he pushed up on his elbows and surged into Lyssie, so deep she gasped. Then she was right there with him, meeting every thrust, going wild beneath him as they both held nothing back.

She cried out, coming hard. Hunt claimed her mouth as he buried his cock balls-deep in her and released in fiery bliss. What started as a sexy bet between them had shifted into something Hunt couldn't even name.

Chapter Thirteen

Hunt eyed the waiter coming into the private room of the exclusive Jinx restaurant in Malibu. He and Cooper had cleared three waiters to work the room, and there were Jinx bouncers checking on them in the kitchens and private hallway. This place took the security of their high-end patrons seriously. Cooper hovered outside the opened doors leading to the deck overlooking the ocean. They had Lyssie covered, but Hunt couldn't shake his uneasiness.

Madden wasn't predictable and that made him tenser than usual. Setting up Maxine by having her arrested showed just how dangerous the prick was.

Lyssie refused to let him control how she lived. She'd offered to not come to the birthday party to not be a distraction or put anyone else in danger, but Maxine had had none of that. Lyssie's friend had a bloodthirsty revenge vibe going on after her arrest and wanted Madden destroyed while she had a front row seat. Hunt liked her.

A server came in with a dome-covered plate. "Miss Brooks, where would you like this?"

"I'll take it, thank you." Lyssie stood up.

What was she doing? Automatically, he cupped her elbow and rose with her. She looked drop-dead gorgeous with streaks of silver shimmering in her curling dark hair that matched her sheath dress. The dress ended mid-thigh, leaving her wickedly long legs bare down to some killer shoes. She managed those four-inch-plus heels with skill, probably had had lots of practice, but he still had the compulsion to keep his hand on her in case she stumbled.

Alyssa took the plate and looked around the table filled with laughing and drinking people, including the birthday girl, Maxine. The rest of the guests consisted of Maxine's mom, brother, his girlfriend and a slew of relatives and friends. "Excuse me, I'll be right back. Please keep eating." She turned to him. "You too. I'll be safe, I'm just taking this to Cooper."

Oh hell, this he had to see. Hunt eased the heavy dish from her hands. "What's in here?"

"I didn't know what he liked, so I ordered three selections, a beef, fish and chicken. Hope he likes something in there." She reached for the plate.

Shifting it to one hand, he put his palm on her back. "Let's go ask him." He led her past the two long tables out into the cool air scented with the ocean and the burning torches.

"What's up?" Cooper asked.

Alyssa jumped.

Hunt wrapped his fingers around her hip to steady her. "Easy. It's just Coop." The other man moved swiftly, but

Hunt had seen him glide up next to them.

"Oh, sorry." She pressed a hand over her chest. "I didn't see you."

"Lucky you," Coop muttered, staying back in the shadows.

Hunt stiffened, old regrets skidding into his chest. The torchlight flickered over Coop's tall, rangy frame. He had on black camo pants, a T-shirt, and a windbreaker to cover his gun. The scar running from his jaw to his eye, mixed with that dead look in his hard gaze, usually had people avoiding him.

Lyssie took the covered plate from Hunt and held it out to Coop. "You scared the server when he tried to get your order."

Coop stilled, his attention flicking down to the serving tray then up. "I told him no. Can't help it if the word no scares the dude."

"Probably it was the 'Get the fuck away from me' that did the trick."

Hunt choked on a laugh.

Coop tilted his head. "You were listening."

"Half the room heard it." She balanced the plate and lifted the lid. "If this doesn't work, I can order something else. They make a great rib eye taco. Would you rather have that?" She shifted slightly, clearly anxious to make Coop happy in spite of her tough-girl attitude.

He raised his eyebrows, but one side of his lean face didn't quite match the other. Nerve damage.

Lyssie held up the plate. "I didn't tell the server it was for you so he probably didn't spit in it."

Coop glanced at Hunt, half his face pulled up in a grin.

"Fine, but no damn waiter better bring me fancy ass cake, especially if it's chocolate." He took the plate gently, as if afraid to touch Alyssa.

She crossed her arms and tapped her foot. "I'll bring you the cake myself and you'll thank me for it."

That was his girl. When he introduced her to Coop, there'd been the usual flicker of surprise and sympathy on her face, then it was gone. She started talking away to Coop, somehow getting him to tell her he'd flown choppers in the Marines and she was all over that, trying to talk him into teaching her how to fly a helicopter. Coop scoffed at her.

Lyssie had started torturing him, asking if he was afraid she'd be better than him at flying.

Jesus, Hunt had nearly split a gut laughing at Coop's expression. Most people were afraid of him, or at least wary. Not her. As Alyssa started inside, Hunt scanned the deck. No one was out here yet since they were just finishing dinner. "Any trouble?"

"No, and nothing from the men watching Madden."

He nodded and caught up with Lyssie before she got to the table, stopping her. Curious, he said, "You haven't asked about Coop's face."

She looked up. "If I want to know, I'll ask him. I have enough people discussing me like they have a right to dissect and judge my life, to amuse themselves with my personal heartbreaks. I won't do that to your friend. His scars are his story to tell if he chooses."

Transfixed by the passion coloring her skin and making her eyes glow, he touched her cheek. "That's what you're doing with your photography, videos and Streets of Valor website, letting people tell their own stories of their scars."

She leaned into his hand. "I hope so." They walked back to their seats.

"Alyssa," Maxine called out. "My mom doesn't believe that story about the two reporters who snuck into the party on campus."

Hunt looked over at Alyssa. "College?"

She nodded and turned to Maxine's mom across the table. "It's true. They were from RevealPop. They looked young, dressed down and got into a frat party Maxine dragged me to. No idea how they knew I was there. But they cornered me outside."

Hunt stiffened. "Were you alone?"

"Yeah. It was hot and smelled like beer in the house, so I went outside and they started taking pictures."

Maxine's mom pushed her plate back and leaned across the table. "It really happened? Maxine chased them off?"

Alyssa laughed. "With pepper spray. She kicked off her shoes and chased them, shouting specific threats to their manly parts. A bunch of guys saw her, and started chasing the reporters too. One of them got their camera and erased the pictures." She shook her head then said to her assistant, "You idiot, you could have been hurt."

Her mom nodded. "Maxine, why didn't you call campus security?"

"I wanted to test my pepper spray. The way one guy was crying, I think it worked."

Hunt half listened while watching the servers clear the tables. He loved that Lyssie was having fun, but that edge kept riding him. What would Madden do?

"After that," cut in Jeff, Maxine's brother, "a group of us guys walked the girls to and from their dorm. I hadn't realized who Alyssa was, but after that I got up to speed. Maxine should have come and gotten me."

Maxine frowned at him. "What for?"

"To save your ass. The usual. Just like I had to bail you out of jail this week." He sighed heavily.

Alyssa stiffened next to him.

Hunt glanced over. "Give it up, princess. He's not taking your money for getting his sister out of jail." Lyssie and Jeff had gone at it yesterday about that. Hunt had learned something—this family cared about Alyssa, not her money and fame.

Jeff laughed. "Alyssa doesn't like to lose."

Hunt grinned at her. "Nope, and she cheats to win." Then he grunted when she elbowed him.

Leaning across the table, she said to Jeff, "It's my fault Maxine got arrested."

"You put that shit in her car and called the cops?"

Lyssie opened her mouth to argue when her phone began frantically buzzing on the table. She picked it up, thumbed the screen, and paled.

Adrenaline slammed through him. "What?"

"Nate. He sent me a link to RevealPop."

• • •

Don't do it. She didn't want to click the link. The last text Nate sent had been Maxine getting arrested followed up by the vile threats in the phone call.

Hunt slid his warm hand beneath her hair to cup her nape. "Here, let me—"

"No." She had to do this, had to be strong enough.

Maxine was here, Eli and his family safe. What else could happen?

"Alyssa."

Her assistant's eyes darted down to her phone then back up. "Is this you on RevealPop?"

A roar filled her ears, turning all the voices around her into white noise. What had Nate done? He had Maxine's cell number. Had he texted her the same link? Her hands shook as she cradled her phone and hit the link.

Others around the table were pulling out their phones, probably loading RevealPop.

Finally the image materialized and the room tilted sickeningly. Nausea erupted in her stomach. *No, no, no.* There was no denying the picture of Alyssa at seventeen, her hair scraped back in a ponytail, her face puffy, tired from the delivery, and in her arms was Eli. Her baby boy. That was the one single picture she had before she gave him up.

Gave him away forever.

Scrolling the screen, she saw the headline. *Breaking news! Alyssa Brooks had a baby at seventeen! Gave him up for adoption!* Nausea boiled in her stomach as she saw a second picture, the one Nate had shown her on his phone. That headline read, *Is Alyssa stalking the family who adopted him?* A quick scan said the family had been forced to flee their home from harassment and were now hiding in an unknown location.

Her phone slid from her nerveless fingers, clattering to the table. Everyone stared at her, even the servers had pulled out their phones. Nate. He'd done this. Not only had he exposed her secret, but he twisted everything to make it seem like she was stalking her son.

"Fuck." Hunt snarled low and mean. He wrapped his arm around her, pulling her close. "Lyssie, you have to breathe." Tucking his fingers beneath her chin, he tilted her head back. "Eyes on me. You're holding your breath."

She was? "Eli," she croaked out. Icy chills broke out on her arms, making her tremble. "What if his parents believe it?"

"Stop it," he said. "Pull it together. We have to get you out of here." Hunt pulled back, slid off his sports coat and wrapped it around her. "Stay here for a second."

Grabbing his arm, her gaze caught on his shoulder holster with the ugly-looking gun tucked into it. She shook it off. "Where are you going?"

"I have to talk to Coop. This is going to unleash more media and batshit crazies on you. It just takes one person to tweet that they saw Alyssa Brooks at Jinx and the media will descend."

She forced herself to let go of him, struggling to control the sick panic flooding her. "Okay."

Hunt vanished out on the deck.

The stony silence pounded at her side from all the guests at the tables. She didn't know where to look, what to say. Her deepest pain was displayed on RevealPop for everyone to discuss over coffee or a beer.

Maxine dropped into Hunt's empty seat and took her hand. "Why didn't you tell me you had a baby? Was this after you lost your mom?"

The betrayal in her friend's eyes was like the betrayal she'd seen in Erin's. How many people was Alyssa going to hurt? "I didn't tell anyone until Nate. Then he threatened him."

Anger chased out the look of betrayal in Maxine. "That slimy bastard. Swear to God, I'm going to neuter him with kitchen shears."

"Not if I get to him first." Hunt returned, reached down, and cupped Alyssa's elbow. "We're going through the kitchen. Cooper's bringing the car around back."

Maxine stood up and hugged her. "I'm a phone call or text away."

"That helps, thank you." Releasing her, she added, "I want you all to stay and celebrate. It's your favorite cake, chocolate raspberry." The restaurant already had her credit card, so that wouldn't be a problem.

Maxine compressed her lips, her expression mutinous. "I'm not—"

"Yes, you are." Leaning into Hunt's hand on her back, she lifted her chin. "Nate won't break me. He won't." Determination gave her the strength she needed right now. She said to her friend, "You and I will be fine. We'll talk tomorrow and I'll explain. Tonight, you party."

"We have a couple guys here keeping watch. You'll be safe, but you don't go home, Maxine, understood? Stay at Jeff's," said Hunt. His hand on her back tightened. "Let's roll."

They headed down a back hallway, with two Jinx security guys flanking them so that Alyssa was in the center. Grateful, she let them guide her, keeping her shielded at the same time. They passed through a hot kitchen bursting with energy, cooking sounds and chatter, and stopped at a thick door.

"Stay here." Hunt went out the door, she assumed to check the alley, then a minute later ducked back in. "Let's go." The two guys followed them out into a wide alleyway. It was completely dark, but wall-mounted lights spilled down pools of illumination. Hunt's Jeep idled less than a dozen feet away with Cooper in the driver's seat.

She wanted to go home and crawl into her bed, or better yet go back to Sonoma and hide there. She'd meant it that she'd be okay, but tonight, she just needed—

A loud roaring noise startled her. Lights flooded the alleyway, coming right at them.

"Go." Hunt shoved her toward the car.

Alyssa's heel caught in the uneven asphalt. She stumbled, windmilling her arms, struggling to keep from falling. The dizzy sensation of nothing being there to stop her descent further threw off her balance. She began to tumble. The roar grew. Lights brightened.

Hunt's hands clamped around her waist, catching her before she slammed into the ground. Alyssa jerked her head to the right.

"Oh." Two headlights came barreling at them. Not a car but two motorcycles.

"Shit. RevealPop," one of the security guys said.

They were barreling down on them, their helmet-mounted cameras running. They were known for their trick riding while filming, so fast and nimble that they got their footage and were gone before anyone could stop them.

Hunt lifted Alyssa off her feet, swung her around, and pushed her toward the door. She stumbled, slamming her knee then shoulder into the wall before another security guard caught her. "Easy there."

Pain ripped into her knee and her shoulder ached. "I'm okay." Her shoes were making her klutzy. Leaning back, she ripped off her thousand-dollar Louboutins.

Cooper flew out of the car, and chased down a photographer on the back of a third motorcycle that had stopped to get still shots. When Coop got close, the bike roared off.

RevealPop had this down to a science.

"Get inside, Lyssie," Hunt snarled. "Now."

She really should listen to Hunt. Everyone knew the trick riders made at least two passes. "You come in with me." His back bulged beneath his T-shirt and shoulder holster, his legs were spread, his hands loose at his sides.

Not a single finger twitched.

"Inside now."

He didn't look back, just snapped the order much like when they'd been at the cliffs. She knew the drill, but normally he'd get her inside himself, not wait out here. Something felt off. Her entire body went on alert.

Sniper mode.

"Miss Brooks—"

One of the two other security guards tugged her arm toward the opened door.

Automatically she took a step, but the second her foot hit the ground fire shot up her right knee. She yelped, shifting her weight off the leg.

Hunt spun.

Even in the vaporous light, Alyssa saw the ice-cold rage in his eyes. His stare dropped to her knee then to the man holding her arm and back to her face. Beneath his jacket gooseflesh popped out on her arms, her body twanged at the rage in him.

He took a step, reaching for her, no doubt to drag her into the kitchen.

Alyssa cringed back, gritting her teeth. "Wait." Her knee, damn it. When she tried to put weight on it, it cramped. Leaning back against the wall, she held up her hand. She needed a minute.

Three riders roared back down the alley.

Cooper jumped back in the idling Jeep, gunned the engine, and swung it into an angle that blocked off Alyssa, forcing the riders to swerve. At the same second, Hunt leaped toward her, throwing his body over hers against the wall. He didn't hurt her, just pinned her there, keeping her covered.

Once the sound of the motorcycles faded away, she shoved him. "Move." Her knee hurt, her shoulder twinged, and she was damned sick of this whole night.

Hunt stepped back, reaching to steady her, but Alyssa ignored him. She had dropped her shoes at some point, but didn't care. She limped to the back of the Jeep idling three steps away, yanked open the door and got in, careful of her stupid knee.

Hunt followed her, easily lifting her and settling her in the other seat. Another guy shut the door and tapped the car in that universal signal of *all clear, go*. Hunt reached past her, grabbed the seat belt and secured her in it.

Coop tore out of the alley. "Where to? Alyssa's house or does she need a doctor? You threw her into that wall pretty hard."

The dome light snapped on, flooding the car. Hunt touched her knee. "Fuck. Hospital. Her leg is bleeding and swelling."

Alyssa leaned forward. "It's not that bad. It's only a cut. I'm not going to the hospital." They were over-reacting. She lifted her gaze to Hunt. "It's not your fault. My stupid shoes, I tripped and you pulled me out of the path of that motorcycle." God, she wouldn't blame him. "You saved me."

"I threw you into a goddamned wall." He reached under the seat, digging out a first aid kit.

Oh, he was not doing this, not now. "I *tripped* into the goddamned wall. You didn't throw me." She leaned forward until her face was right up in his. "Don't mistake me for Rachel. I'm not scared of you."

. . .

"You cringed." *Hell. Shut up.* She'd had a bad enough night, he didn't need to dump his shit on her. If she didn't want him to touch her, he wouldn't, except to protect her and get her knee to stop bleeding. He tore open the medicated wipes and carefully swabbed at the cut.

It wasn't too bad, probably wouldn't need stitches, but the knee had some swelling, redness and was a little warm to the touch. She'd definitely banged it up. They were absolutely going to the hospital and getting her checked out. Adrenaline was a powerful drug and could mask serious pain for the short term.

Cold hands landed on his cheeks and pulled his face to hers. "I wasn't scared, I was in pain and pissed, and I'm upset. That picture..." Tears welled in her eyes. "Those were my moments with Eli. Mine. They were all I had of him before he became someone else's child." Tears spilled down her face. "And now they're saying I'm the one stalking him. It's too much."

Her tears ripped his chest wide open. Hunt burned with hatred for Madden. What the fuck was his game here?

Destroying Lyssie in the media? What would that gain him?

For a few seconds out there in that alley, Hunt had thought it was a hit, but no, just asshole paparazzi. Tossing down the wipes, Hunt slid next to her and wrapped his arm around her. "I'm sorry, baby. I wish I could undo it."

"You didn't do it, Nate did. He obviously found my computer file of Eli's pictures and stole that. I never showed anyone that picture. It was mine." She turned into him.

Hunt held her close, rubbing her back through his jacket. She wasn't crying really. The tears were more of an overflow from what he could feel.

"Almost there," Coop said. "No tail, no trouble so far."

Hunt nodded, then glanced down Lyssie's legs. "What'd you do with your shoes?"

"I took them off when I kept tripping. Stupid shoes."

She sounded so disgruntled that he smiled despite their shitty night. "They looked sexy."

"You wear them then. They pissed me off."

Coop snorted in the front. "I'd pay to see that."

Hunt ignored him and stroked Lyssie's hair. As long as she let him hold her, touch her, the cold burn in his veins eased up. They'd get her looked at and then take her home to figure out Madden's game.

"You're pissing me off too, Cooper."

Hunt caught Coop's surprise in the rearview mirror.

"What'd I do?"

"Told Hunt he threw me into the wall. I tripped. On my stupid ass shoes. From now on, I'm wearing ballet slippers. No one trips in ballet slippers."

Tilting her head up, Hunt saw her tears had dried. "Who isn't pissing you off?"

"You're not, now that you know I'm not Rachel."

Glancing around, he saw they were turning into the hospital. "Yeah, I think that's about to change."

"Why?" She looked around, then glared at him. "No. I'm not going."

"Yeah, you are."

Chapter Fourteen

This couldn't be happening, not again. Alyssa sipped the water the nurse had brought her. Hunt and Coop were down the hall talking to hospital security, trying to keep a lid on Alyssa being there.

Her knee didn't need stitches, just a couple butterfly bandages and ice to minimize swelling and bruising. The doctor had looked at her shoulder and it was fine, too. She'd just be sore for a couple days. Ice, heat, the usual. Not a big deal. But this? Yeah, this was big. Astounding. Alyssa looked at the doctor, conceding that she certainly looked competent. But still, she had to ask, "Pregnant? You're sure?"

"You said your period is late, that's why I ran the test."

"Well yeah, but...I lost track of time. I hadn't even thought about it until you asked."

They'd wanted to do a precautionary x-ray on her knee, which prompted the inquiries about her last period. She'd had to look at her phone calendar to figure out that she was late. "Wait, I had the birth control shot."

"Nearly four months ago according to what you told me. They are only good for twelve weeks."

Damn. Alyssa hadn't been careless since Eli was born, but she'd thought she and Nate were marrying and planned to start a family right away. She'd screwed up. Again. The very first time she had sex with Hunt, they'd forgotten the condom.

Unbelievable. What was wrong with her? She was a woman with an education and money, and she couldn't figure out how to stop getting knocked up. Even better, she found out the night it was revealed to the world that she'd had Eli and given him up.

Hunt would hate her, never trust her again, and yet, underneath all that, there was a tiny kernel of hope dancing and popping in her stomach, waiting to explode into joy. A baby. A child.

Pregnant.

She'd only been with Hunt a few weeks. Glancing up, she said, "It's only been two weeks since we started having sex." Too shocked to be embarrassed, she dug her hand into the bedsheet of the private room they had her stashed in to keep her out of sight.

"Since this is your second child, your HCG hormone levels rise faster, and the pregnancy tests today are more sensitive. Two weeks is enough time to show positive." The doctor studied her face. "If this isn't something you want, Miss Brooks, I can direct you to an exclusive—"

"No." The word erupted from her throat. This baby was hers. But Hunt... Oh God, what would she tell him? How would he react?

The woman touched her shoulder. "You're barely pregnant. This has clearly been a shock on top of a rough night. You don't have to rush into any decisions, just take it easy on your knee for a week, and see an obstetrician in the next month."

The kindness in the other woman's eyes helped calm her a bit. "Thank you. That makes sense. I'm a little stunned."

"I gathered that. Women are surprised by pregnancies all the time. That's the beauty of having eight or nine months to get it sorted out. Just take a deep breath." Dropping her hand, she said, "Anything else you need? How are your knee and shoulder feeling?"

"Okay. I'm more tired than anything."

"Hormones and adrenaline crash. We'll see if we can get you out of here and home." Moving the ice, she examined her knee again. "I can write you a prescription for a safe painkiller, but a hot bath, more ice and some Tylenol should do it."

"I'll be fine with that."

"Good." She replaced the ice, then smiled at her. "Congratulations."

The doctor left, leaving her in the quiet room with just her breathing. A baby. A child.

Hunt's baby.

Would he be upset? Or happy? She'd find out when she told him, but she wasn't ready for that. Not yet.

The one thing she knew for sure was that she wasn't giving up this child.

• • •

Alyssa woke up to an empty bed. A glance at her night-stand clock told her it was hovering around four a.m. She tested her right shoulder. Barely sore. Her knee throbbed a bit more but her biggest problem was a full bladder. Slowly she got up, went to the bathroom, returned to take a couple Tylenol, and then settled in bed. Moving around had eased her knee.

Hunt's side of the bed was ice cold. He had to be down in the studio. A nightmare? A part of her wanted to go check on him.

No. You gave him the room for his studio so he could have his own space. You promised him.

She hated him alone like that, but at the same time, she respected that he needed his space. Like she liked to run alone.

Soft footsteps sounded. In the moonlight she saw him move around her side of the bed. "You okay?"

"You knew I was awake?" A wave of emotion moved through her chest, drowning out years of loneliness. Right after her mom died, while pregnant, she'd been so alone, cry-ing many nights and secretly hoping Parker would hear her and care enough to notice. He hadn't. But Hunt cared. She understood that he might not be able to love her and stay with her, but he cared enough to come upstairs and check on her.

"Heard the toilet." The mattress sank as he sat.

The silvery moonlight showed his rumpled hair, wide shoulders and arms wrapped in ink, down to his flat, ripped stomach. He'd pulled on a pair of running shorts when he'd gotten up. Alyssa settled her hand on his warm, heavily mus-cled thigh. She loved touching him; it was part desire and part sheer need. "I'm fine. How about you? Had a nightmare?"

The sound of the waves outside her French doors and their co-mingled breathing filled the room. Finally he answered, "Yeah."

"Did sculpting help?"

He dropped a hand on the mattress and leaned in, blocking out the world. "Are you worrying about me?"

"I care about you. No matter what happens, I will always care." She needed him to know that. "So did sculpting help? Do you want to go back down there? I'm fine."

"It helped." He brushed her hair back. "But you're what I need right now."

That surprised her, causing her to suck in a breath. He'd been so careful once they'd gotten home from the hospital even though she really wasn't hurt bad. "You want sex?"

Hunt caught her fingers in his. "I always want you. It was hell to help you out of your dress when we got home and into the tub, and not touch you in the way I wanted to, but that's not happening right now. I want, shit, no I need to take care of you." He brushed his thumb over her lips. "You weren't scared of me. For a second I thought you were cringing back against that wall from me."

"No."

He slid the pad of his thumb across the tip of her tongue. "I know that now. You trust me and I need this. Let me care for you." At her nod, he said, "I'm going to turn on the light, close your eyes."

Alyssa relaxed into the pillows and slid her eyelids shut.

The light snapped on and Hunt tugged the covers off her. "Swelling's down." His fingers moved gently over her knee, around the cut.

"It wasn't that bad. I've done worse twisting my knee while running. There was just that shock of pain when I hit it. Like hitting your funny bone in your elbow."

He lifted her leg and slid a pillow under it, then covered her and the light went off, freeing her to open her eyes. The bed dipped on the other side, and Hunt pressed up against her side and wrapped his arms around her. "When we get up later this morning, we need to go online and order you some big ugly pajamas if I'm going to keep my hands off you. That little T-shirt and panties are just cruel."

The thick enticing ridge of his hard-on pressed against her hip. "We could take them off." She knew he'd be gentle with her when she needed him to.

He kissed her. "Tonight I just want to hold you." Shifting, he pressed her head against his chest. "Talk to me. Tell me why you're awake. Thinking about Eli?"

"Some."

"We're going to prove Madden did all this, not you."

She nodded, having to believe it. "I just feel so exposed. I hate it. That picture of me and Eli, it was my only moment with him. The nurse took the picture for me. It was mine. I didn't want to share it."

Hunt laid his palm on her cheek. "I get it. There are things, one thing in particular, I never want anyone to know."

"Like what's in your locked studio in Sonoma?"

"Worse. I can't even put it in clay. The thing that proves I really am a killer."

His tortured words from the cabin bounced in her head: *What really scares me is that one day I could flip that switch and not be able to turn it off.*

"The man who protected me in the alley last night,

forced me to go to the hospital, then took care of me when we got home is not a cold killer." She could see the doubt in his eyes. What had happened to make him believe that?

Could he ever get past it enough to be a father to their child?

. . .

Hunt was shocked he slept late. After showering, he found Lyssie downstairs, sitting at her white antique desk in her little office, staring at the computer screen.

God she was beautiful. No makeup, her hair clipped up and a soft expression on her face as she stared at the computer. Unable to resist the allure of Lyssie, he went to her.

She jumped. "Oh, I didn't hear you."

He tilted her chin up and kissed her. She tasted of toothpaste and coffee. "Did you ever go back to sleep?"

"Not really. I came down here to work and get my mind off everything. I finished the tribute video for your parents."

Turning to look, he expected to see the video. Instead, it was a news site with the photo of Lyssie and Eli as a newborn.

"What's Nate's game? What good does releasing all of this do? I mean, yeah, he's making me look bad…" She sighed, waving to the screen. Tension chased off the softness in her expression. "The comments are ugly and the press is descending like vultures. This isn't like having a thug hurt a dog to lure me out and almost hit me as a warning, or setting up Maxine and saying he'll drop the charges if I do what he says. Those were meant to terrify me into compliance. This is…something else."

Yeah, they were all trying to figure out Madden's motive.

"He's lashing out the only way he can, or it's his plan B." Either way, this guy was a loaded gun. "Whatever his game, it may have backfired on him. That's the reason I was looking for you."

"How?"

"I just got off the phone with Adam. Tami Nash called him, she saw all the coverage." Hunt touched the screen with the picture of Lyssie and Eli. "This picture got to her. She said she can't do it anymore, can't keep covering for Madden. The night his mom died, he left her house and was gone for nearly two hours. She's asked Adam to help her make sure her sister is safe then she's going to the police today. This is the break we need; it's all going to start unraveling for Madden."

Staring at the picture, Lyssie blinked. "This picture did it? Why?"

"She knows what it's like to be terrorized with threats against someone you love. Your son for you, and for Tami, her sister. In this picture you're so damned young and vulnerable, your heart breaking in your eyes as you held the child you were going to give up." He shifted his gaze to the screen, and it punched him hard. She'd done something so loving and strong, yet brutally painful, and it was all there in that image. "This..." He touched the screen again. "Is your story and Tami was moved by it. Lyssie, it made you real to her."

She swallowed, her gaze sliding into his. "Really? Just from the picture?"

Hunt's chest clenched at the emotion riding her expression, hope surging up over her pain. "Isn't that what you're going to do with your site? Show real people in their valiant moments? That moment when you chose what was best for Eli over what was best for you, that's your valiant moment and people will see it, Lyssie. Even if most of them don't, I do and people like Tami do. You're helping her have her own valiant moment."

Leaning closer, she kissed him then rested her forehead against his. "Thank you, Hunt. For everything. I was so scared after Nate threatened Eli. I didn't know where else to go and ran to you. I hated that you'd see me so weak and foolish but—"

He caught her hair, easing her head back. "Is that what you think I see?" Didn't she understand? Lyssie was the beautiful strong princess. "If your knee is up to it, I want to show you something." He stood and held out his hand, giving her the choice.

She put her soft hand in his without a second's hesitation. After tugging her gently to her feet, he led her across the hall and to the door of his studio. Every time he came to this door, a wave of emotion gripped him. Another thing Lyssie gave him—his art and the freedom to deal with his nightmares his own way without judgment. Taking a breath, he pushed open the door to show her what he'd been working on in the night.

"Oh." She went to the spinning table and circled the sculpture. "Who is this? Why is she so fierce?"

"It's rough yet, but it's you." Hunt wrapped his arms around her.

"Me? Fierce?" She twisted her head to see him. "That's how you see me?"

"Lyssie, most people are afraid of Coop."

"Because of a scar? That's ridiculous. It's not even that

bad."

"Because he's a scary SOB with anger issues and he doesn't care if he lives or dies."

"You care," she said softly. "He's your friend."

That right there was one of the things that gut-punched him. "You're sweet and fierce, and you treated him like a capable man, not with pity or derision. You see him as a real person."

"Because he is. He's more than his scars, Hunt."

"Fierce, baby girl. Right now your eyes are glinting with it." Putting his arms around her from behind, he said, "After we went to sleep, I kept jerking awake, hearing you yelp, or seeing you flinch when I reached for you."

"I told you—"

"Hush," he said into her hair. "It's a dream. Anyway, I knew I wasn't going to sleep and came down here to sculpt. I thought I'd do something dark, but instead of that need to vent, I saw you leaning into my face, saying, 'I'm not Rachel.' I had to capture that image." He'd been down here for hours, just letting the feel of the clay and the drive to carve out Lyssie's beauty calm and center him. It wasn't venting; it was creating.

She gripped his arm and looked up at him. "What does that mean?"

"That you're helping me see myself as more than a killer." He held his hands out in front of her. "My hands can create beauty again."

Lyssie linked her fingers with his.

"I don't know if it's enough. Last night when those motorcycles got too close to you, I tossed you behind me and my first instinct was to reach for my gun. I was pissed, enraged, not cold like I normally am when I go into sniper mode, but hot." With her in his arms, this was easier to talk about.

She squeezed his hands.

"When this is over and things settle down—"

She craned her head up. "Hunt, this is my life. That stuff last night? It's not usually so dramatic, but this is who I am. You keep worrying that I can't handle your secret. The thing that tortures you with some kind of guilt." Unlinking their hands, she turned and faced him. Her eyes blazed with a heart-stopping combination of strength and vulnerability. "What I worry is that you can't handle this. My real life."

Hell. He opened his mouth when the doorbell rang.

"Speaking of my real life, that's Maxine. I promised I'd tell her about Eli."

. . .

Dragon Wing Productions' office was quiet and empty on Sunday morning. Alyssa felt strange being there after walking out nearly a month ago. So much had changed, and now she was back, heading through the parking garage to the private elevator on her slightly stiff knee with Hunt, Detective Ryan Zahn and a couple young uniforms, one of whom had a video camera. *Surreal.* Once inside the elevator, she blurted out, "The media followed us. Nate's going to know we're here."

The detective shrugged. "You're half owner of the company, you've given us permission to search. If Mr. Madden shows up, he's welcome to cooperate and answer questions."

Alyssa would think the man was callous and bored,

except for the glint of determination in his light brown eyes. The same detective that investigated Nate's mother's fall had always believed Nate had something to do with it. Tami Nash had gone to him, formally recanting her alibi for Nate. She turned over all the pictures and evidence she had that showed Nate used her younger sister to blackmail her into silence. Detective Zahn was determined to build a case. Alyssa had also told him everything that had happened with her and Nate. They just needed some evidence linking Nate.

Hunt took her hand in his. "Cooper is watching Madden too."

Right. Okay. They had no way of knowing if Nate knew Tami had gone to the police so Hunt's boss, Adam, was protecting her and her sister. If they found some evidence today, then this could end soon.

The doors opened with a soft swish to the round reception area with the Dragon Wing logo on soft gray-lavender walls, and elegant couches and chairs around a sleek coffee table on a carpet.

The detective stopped at another wall with a life-sized framed screen shot of a scene from her mother's movie *Cry for Melissa*. "She was beautiful and talented."

Alyssa paused as the familiar wave of grief and nostalgia washed over her. "And a great mom," she added softly. Just like Alyssa was determined to be. She hadn't told Hunt yet. The thought of it caused her stomach to cramp with anxiety, but she would tell him once she confirmed it with her doctor this week and things calmed down. Staring up into her mom's eyes, she knew she was ready and strong enough this time to be this child's mom.

Hunt squeezed her hand.

The detective turned to face her. "She died too young in a tragic accident, but what happened to Madden's mother wasn't an accident. That case has dogged me for four years. I knew that cocky SOB had come into the house the night before." He grimaced. "The neighbor told us Lorelei always bought this fancy water that came in four-packs for him. She'd just gone shopping that day. We found the grocery receipt and sure enough, she'd bought it that day, but one of the waters was missing from the four-pack in her fridge. The empty wasn't in any of her trash cans or anywhere in the house. That drove me out of my mind. I knew Madden had been there, that he'd pushed his mother down the stairs, grabbed a water and left her to die. I didn't have enough evidence, and his girlfriend at the time, Miss Nash, wouldn't crack on the alibi." The man's jaw flexed. "Then Madden collected the life insurance money and lived the high life. The next thing I know, he's dating you. Thought he was smart and untouchable."

"Tami didn't know what Nate was going to do before he left, right?"

He shook his head. "Madden told her he was going out to grab some food for breakfast. When he returned, he told her if the police ever asked, he was there all night, that they'd watched a movie until eleven thirty and went to sleep. The next morning when the police came, she began to put it together. Later she asked him where he'd really been."

She almost didn't want to ask. Hunt stood quietly by her, holding her hand, the other two officers standing back a few feet. "What did he say?"

"That he took care of a problem. Then he warned Miss Nash not to become a problem."

A shudder wracked her shoulders. "That's what he said to me, right there in that elevator. 'I eliminate problems. Don't be a problem, Alyssa.'"

Hunt put his arm around her shoulders, his solid warmth calming her. She thought of that sculpture of her that Hunt was working on, the one where he called her fierce. Time to be fierce. "Let's see what we can do about eliminating Nate's freedom. This way." She led the men down the hallway, passing her stepfather's office and coming to Nate's. She used her master keycard to lead them inside.

One of the officers began videotaping as the detective said, "Miss Brooks, do you give us permission to search the office of Mr. Nate Madden, vice president of business and legal affairs at Dragon Wing Productions?"

"Yes."

After quickly showing them around, Hunt took her arm. "Lyssie, come sit down." He led her to the leather couch in the reception area of Nate's office.

"I'm fine."

Tugging her down next to him, he said, "The doctor told you to take it easy on your knee for a week or so."

Okay, she had to admit it didn't suck that he was concerned. "It's not bad, just a little tight, only sore when I bump or twist it. It's weird to be back here. So much has changed."

He threaded their fingers together. "Yeah?"

"I left that day so angry, betrayed and lost." Would this last between her and Hunt? They'd only been together less than a month, and her pregnancy was going to throw a huge curveball into their budding relationship. Part of her wanted to tell him now, to just blurt it out.

Yeah, good plan. Shock the hell out of him right here

where her ex-fiancé's office is being searched by a detective and an officer, while being filmed by another cop. *Not the time.* Instead, she kept it simple. "I don't feel lost anymore. I'm more sure of who I am and what I want." She wanted Hunt and their baby, but if Hunt decided that's not what he wanted, Alyssa and their child would be okay. Oh, a part of her heart would break, the part that Hunt had always owned, but she'd survive, be the best mom she could and she'd never stop Hunt from seeing his child. "I hope they find something today and—"

"Alyssa. What the hell is going on?"

Jerking her head around, she saw her stepfather in the doorway, his eyes scanning the room. Parker's golf shirt and slacks suggested he'd been at the club.

Hunt rose, easing Alyssa to her feet.

Parker's eyes narrowed on Hunt then swiveled back to her. "What have you done now? I don't even know you anymore. You quit, ran away, took up with some random man from your past, and I find out in the media about a baby you had that I knew nothing about? A baby?" He blinked rapidly as if it was incomprehensible. "Now you were filmed coming in the offices with cops."

"I told you what was going on when I called you weeks ago after overhearing that you paid Nate to get me to marry him. I told you then Nate threatened me and you insisted I was over-reacting. What I didn't tell you that day, because I no longer trusted you, was that Nate also threatened my son. He's the one that put those pictures out in the media, not me. In the last three weeks, Nate's tried to terrorize me by having someone threaten my son, sending some thug to nearly run me over with a car, and having my assistant falsely arrested."

Strain dug in around Parker's eyes, aging him in seconds. Silence hung between them, then Parker pressed a hand to his forehead. "Nate was so confident he'd get you back until that last set of pictures of you and him"—he waved his hand at Hunt—"came out. Then he was furious. He knew about your baby? I mean, I didn't know, how could I have not known?"

"Because you wouldn't even look at me after Mom died."

"Miss Brooks." Detective Zahn walked out.

Parker strode past him. "I'm Parker Dean, I own—"

"I know who you are, Mr. Dean. My officer at the door called to get my approval to allow you up here. From where I'm standing, it appears you've been at the very least aiding Mr. Madden in stalking and blackmailing your stepdaughter."

Parker froze. "No, that's not—"

"Come with me please. Miss Brooks, you and Hunt as well."

The group went into Nate's office with the glass windows, white floors, and huge mahogany desk. There were dual monitors hooked up to Nate's laptop. Alyssa looked at the screens and felt the blood drain from her face.

Both monitors were filled with pictures. The left one had various shots of Eli playing soccer, riding his bike, getting off his school bus... Nausea boiled up in her stomach.

"Easy, Alyssa." Hunt wrapped his hand around her hip. "Slow breaths."

"Is that the boy?" Parker asked. "My God, he looks like Jenna, lighter colored hair, but his eyes and that mouth..."

He turned, facing the detective. "Nate had all these pictures? There must be a dozen."

"More. That's just one set." The detective gestured to the other monitor. "Those are his other victims. His ex-girlfriend Tami Nash, and her younger sister, Kelly." Hard eyes landed on Parker. "Did you know about this?"

"No! I didn't even know Alyssa had a child. I don't know these other women, well, that one looks like a kid." He rubbed his temples. "What's Nate done? This was all a business deal, just strategy. After Jenna died, the company was sinking. People said I was destroying her legacy. I—"

"Enough." Detective Zahn cut him off. "Here's the deal, Mr. Dean. I need a few hours to get my ducks in a row then Mr. Madden will be arrested. You do not want to warn him and talk to him at all. Not even a text. He reaches out to you, don't respond. Are we clear?"

Turning from the detective, he stared at Alyssa. "It's true? All this? Nate really blackmailed you? Tried to hurt you?"

As angry and hurt as she was, one thing she knew for sure was that her mother had loved him and he'd loved her mom. Jenna's death had changed him. Changed them both, really. For the first time ever, she saw the truth. Parker had crumpled, while Alyssa had found a way to grow and get stronger.

Chapter Fifteen

Hunt was in a hell of a good mood by the time he got home Monday afternoon. He had Madden's arrest on video for Lyssie, but before he could get home to show her, he'd had to go into the office for the paperwork. Sienna was a bear about everything being documented, with good reason, of course. If they were called to court, or their actions questioned by police, they needed detailed records. So Hunt did the reports and now he was home.

In just a few days, he felt nearly as comfortable here in Lyssie's place as at the vineyard. He parked his Jeep in the huge garage, bypassed Lyssie's and Maxine's cars, and headed into the kitchen. After punching in the alarm code, he headed down the stairs. "Lyssie?"

"Down here," she called out.

The sound of her voice tugged at his chest. Definitely home. He found her and Maxine on the couch, both looking exhausted. Bending over, he kissed his girl, then raised his eyebrows. "Tough day being famous?"

She smacked him. "You have no idea, Marine."

Maxine laughed. "We've been inundated with calls, emails, and messages since we released Alyssa's video statement about Eli. Alyssa refuses to discuss Eli beyond what she said in her video, but people are interested in her site."

Hunt sat on the arm. "Yeah?" After some arm-twisting by Maxine, Alyssa had agreed to launch her Streets of Valor website with that video. When he saw it, it'd taken his breath away at the utter power and love she expressed in her decision to give up her son, then her plea for the world to leave him and his family alone.

"We uploaded a few pictures today," Alyssa said. "The response—"

"Crashed the website," Maxine said. Then she turned to Lyssie. "Told you. You were wasting your talent at Dragon Wing. This is what you should be doing."

Lyssie took her assistant's hand. "I couldn't have done it without you."

"I know." Maxine grinned. "You should give me a raise, or at least hazard pay." She got up and said, "I'm beat. I'm going home and will be back in the morning to keep working."

"Not too early," Lyssie said. "I have an appointment at nine."

Hunt cut his gaze to her. "What appointment?"

She didn't quite look at him. "Um, my gynecologist."

Maxine looked as confused as he felt as she pulled out her phone. "It's not on your calendar."

Lyssie stared at her hands. "I made it today and they got me in tomorrow."

Worry gripped his muscles. "Why? What's wrong?"

"Nothing, I need to get that shot, and Nate's in jail now so I figured it's safe enough for me to take care of it."

Shot? That's right, she'd told him she'd been on a birth control shot when they'd forgotten the condom, but she needed it again, so yeah, that shot. "I'll take you."

"You don't have to now. Nate's not a threat and—"

"I'm taking you. The media follows every move you make, especially now with Madden's arrest. It's only going to get more insane. You need protection. Me." He wasn't budging on that.

"And this is where I leave," Maxine said.

Hunt looked up. "Be careful. Are you going home or back to your brother's?"

"Home. Love Jeff but I'm ready to go home."

He understood that. "Text me or Lyssie once you're inside and the security system is on."

Maxine tilted her head. "You know, you're not a bad guy." She left.

Hunt laughed, then dragged Lyssie into his lap and kissed her the right way, deep and thorough. Tasting her, feeling her soften into him, her sweet ass rubbing his cock. Finally breaking apart, he rubbed her swollen bottom lip. "Missed you today."

"I missed you too, but today felt like my first day doing what I love. We put up the pictures of Treva and her dog Sabrina, and they got huge hits. A TV station wants to interview Treva and Sabrina. She Skyped me and is stoked. She's such an amazing young woman."

Her joy infected him with a wave of contentment and desire. This was what he wanted—to come home and talk over his day like a normal person. Hold a woman—this woman—in his arms. "You're happy."

"Very. I couldn't wait for you to get back to tell you."

Shyness crept into her voice. Or was that doubt? He didn't want that between them. "I love hearing about your day, and I couldn't wait to get home and share this with you." Shifting her to get out his cell phone, he cued up the video of Madden being arrested as he left his condo this morning to go to work.

"You can't arrest me!" Madden shouted, his face turning red then purple. The idiot actually shoved the cop after that, which earned him a face plant on the ground, arms wrenched behind his back and cuffed, then he was jerked up to his feet. A thin line of blood dripped from a cut on his lip, and Madden was still bellowing about lawyers and lawsuits.

Detective Zahn calmly told him he was under arrest, read him his rights, and the cops shoved him in the back of a patrol car and drove off.

She craned her head to look up into his eyes. "Unbelievable. He was going to fight that cop." Alyssa shook her head. "That barely looked like the smooth, always-in-control man I knew. He's losing it."

"He knows it's over, and the best part is he knows you refused to let him blackmail or terrorize you. You fought back."

She settled back against him. "You're enjoying this."

Hunt buried his nose in her neck, taking a second to absorb the scent of her skin. "You have no idea. The only thing better would have been shoving my fist into his face, but this worked too." That man never deserved Lyssie, and now that she was his, he'd kill to protect her. No question. Hunt had killed to protect his country and his fellow Marines, but

Lyssie evoked a fierce possession and need to protect that was nearly animalistic.

She turned to straddle him. "It's going to be over soon, isn't it?"

Damn, she was so hot like this, but her words sent up caution flags, making his guts tense. "The case, yes, but *we're* not over, Lyssie." He couldn't lose her.

"I meant the threat from Nate, but since you brought it up, do you want to stay for a while, Hunt?"

He wasn't ready to let her go. "Yes. I want this, Lyssie. Once we're sure you're safe—"

"And Eli and his family."

There it was, his fierce girl with that ability to love even from a distance. He stroked his hand down her belly, touching that ruby dragon tear in the stylized heart peeking out over her pants. "And Eli." That child would always be in her heart. One day he hoped the boy's parents would tell him how special his birth mother is.

Lifting his gaze to hers, he said, "I'll go back to my job, you'll work on your site and charities, and I'll figure out how to take my famous girlfriend out. I want to take you on more dates, then bring you home and make love to you. I want this, Lyssie. For as long as it lasts." He couldn't make her promises beyond that.

"Can we do that last part now?"

Oh, hell yeah. His day got even better.

• • •

You're pregnant.

Having her regular gynecologist confirm the hospital

doctor's findings earlier today made it real. She really was going to have a baby.

Hunt's baby.

Her stomach flipped in agitation. She wanted him to be excited, but what if he wasn't? What if he was angry and felt trapped like Scott had? Well, he'd be home soon, she'd tell him and find out. She finished the salads just as she heard the garage door open. A minute later, the alarm beeped as Hunt came through the door. Damn, he looked fine wearing those oh-so-sexy jeans and a black pullover with the sleeves pushed up. Still wearing his shades, he gave off that slightly dangerous vibe that made her hormones rage.

Tossing his sunglasses on the counter, he wrapped an arm around her waist and kissed her. Raising his head, he said, "Something smells damned good."

"Beef tenderloin with balsamic tomatoes. Hungry? It's in the warming tray."

"Starved." Helping her get dinner on the table, he said, "Madden was arraigned but his bond is a million plus. He's not going to raise that very easily. Parker has sworn not to help him, and he's upside down on his condo, doesn't really have assets. No family. He's screwed."

Alyssa grabbed the salads and some sparkling water then sat next to Hunt. "Most of me is relieved, but there's a small part that's sad. There was a time when I thought we were friends. I cared about the man I thought he was."

Hunt touched her hand. "It's okay to have mixed feelings."

That eased her worries. "No more talk about him tonight. Let's eat before dinner gets cold."

They dug in while the cool ocean breeze flowed in from the open sliding glass door behind her. Hunt ignored his salad and went right for the meat. Amused, she watched as he attacked his dinner. He hadn't been kidding about being hungry.

After a few bites, he said, "This is good, Lyssie."

Warmth flooded her. "Thanks." Recalling something else, she added, "Oh, next week Maxine and I are doing the monthly Superhero Day at the children's hospital."

"What's that?"

"It's a lot of fun. Sometimes I have actors dressed as superheroes, and then we always bring costumes and makeup for the kids with a team to help them dress if they are up to it. We take pics and videos. We stage little scenes, as much as the kids can handle with their illnesses or limitations. They get the pictures and videos." Realizing she was rambling a bit, she tried to focus. "Anyway, I wanted you to know if we're still concerned about security then."

"All right, I'll work it out to provide protection."

Since they agreed to keep seeing each other, they needed to begin figuring it out. For weeks they'd been focused on her, but Hunt had a life too and she wanted to support him as much as he had her. "You can't go with me everywhere indefinitely. Once this thing with Nate settles down, I won't need a bodyguard as often."

He set his fork down. "Once A Marine is growing, you can use them for your bodyguards when I'm not available. I trust them. Good for you and the business."

That worked and she wanted to hear more about his job. "You love what you do, don't you?" She was getting to see another side of him here in L.A.

He buttered another freshly made roll. "In some of my missions as a sniper, I really didn't see the payoff. I might be going after a known terrorist who had killed hundreds and eliminate him. It was cold, removed. I like making a difference on a more personal level."

She forgot her dinner. He so rarely talked about his actual work as a Marine that she was surprised he did now. "Did you ever have other kinds of missions where you saw the payoff?"

He set down his butter knife. "Yes. I cleared buildings and got trapped in gunfire a few times. I was called into hostage situations and people with bombs strapped around them in busy marketplaces. It was...intense."

"You shot into crowds?"

"I've had to do it, yes."

"Were you scared?" Her heart pounded thinking about it.

"Not at the time. Adrenaline usually jacked me up to that state of high functioning awareness. My focus was 100 percent on the job. Emotions can cause mistakes and the wrong people die."

What had he told her at the cabin? *Only in my nightmares, I wasn't cold and in absolute control like I had been in real life. Instead, I felt it all: fear, remorse, hatred and sickness at seeing a man die from my bullet. Even after I woke in a cold sweat, I couldn't stop it unless I sculpted.* All those emotions he'd repressed had surged up. What he'd done was brave, but did he realize how courageous it was to survive the aftermath? To find a way to cope and live with his scars and not lash out at others? To continue to help people with the skills he'd learned?

Alyssa put her hand on his arm. "You're the best man I know, Hunt." However this turned out once she told him she was pregnant, she was going to make sure their child knew that about their father. Whatever role Hunt wanted in the kid's life, she'd support it, no matter how much it hurt if he rejected her. She swallowed. *Tell him.* It was time and she knew it. She tried to gather the words in her mind.

Covering her hand with his, his eyes churned. "You make it easy to talk."

Hunt's phone rang.

He frowned, taking his hand away. "That's Sienna's ringtone. I'd better take it." Getting out his cell, he answered, "What's up?"

The second his eyes hit hers she knew it was bad.

Chapter Sixteen

"Have you seen RevealPop?" Sienna asked.

Hunt tightened his grip on his cell phone. What now? Hadn't Lyssie had enough shocks? "No."

"There's a picture of you and Alyssa coming out of a gynecologist's office."

He relaxed a little bit. "The media is following us everywhere." Yeah it sucked, but as Lyssie said, this was her life.

"Well, if you two are trying to keep her pregnancy a secret, the cat is out of the bag."

Adrenaline burst into his blood stream, jerking him upright. "What?"

"Some asshole took a cell phone picture of her medical records and posted it on RevealPop."

Everything in him went cold. The dining room came into ultra-sharp focus. Even the scents of beef, balsamic and yeasty bread refined. In what felt like slow motion, he turned to Lyssie.

She had her hair in one of those fancy ponytails that lay over her shoulder, her oval face drained of color, making her brown eyes huge and troubled.

She's pregnant?

"I need to go." He disconnected from Sienna.

"Hunt? What is it?"

Ignoring Lyssie's strained question, he called up Reveal-Pop on his phone.

Alyssa Brooks pregnant! Is her bodyguard the daddy?

There was a photo of them from a long-range lens. His face was hard, clearly scanning the area around them. Lyssie wore the same pretty little dress she had on now but the shot was close enough to see the slight slackness in her jaw that showed she wasn't paying attention. Totally distracted.

Pregnant.

The word drummed over and over. *Preg. Nant. Preg. Nant.* Scrolling down, he saw the medical notes for Alyssa Brooks. *Pregnant.*

She'd lied to him. A million thoughts raced through his head, fighting for prominence. He'd trusted Lyssie, cared about her. Helped her. Opened up to her and she'd lied to him. How could he trust her when she withheld something like this? Hell, he'd sat there in her gynecologist's office waiting for her. Uncomfortable as hell, but he'd done it.

"Hunt?"

Fury took precedence. Her distress pulled at him but he shut it down. "When were you going to tell me? What was the plan here, Alyssa?"

She flinched at the way he snapped her name.

Oh, hell no. She didn't get to be scared of him now. "Or was this your plan all along, find someone to knock you up to get that baby you wanted so desperately?"

Confusion and panic swirled in her eyes. "No! But how do you know? I mean…"

He held up his phone, angling his screen so she could see the RevealPop site.

She closed her eyes, her entire body deflating. "It never ends. Now someone stole my medical records."

Damn it, he refused to feel sorry for her. "So it's true. You're pregnant?"

She snapped her head up, clamping her clammy hand on his arm. "I planned to tell you tonight."

Had she? Because how would he know that now? "So I took you to the doctor today to find out if you were pregnant, not for a birth control shot?" He really wanted to get this straight. "Or did you go in there to get the shot and found out?"

She cut her gaze left.

Shit. Hunt slid his arm from her hand and shoved to his feet. "Don't you dare lie to me. Not now." He couldn't look at her. He went to the sliding glass door that opened to the deck overlooking the ocean. The briny damp air breezing in did nothing to clear his head.

"I found out at the hospital on Friday night. They asked me when my last period was, a standard question when women are going to have an x-ray. When they realized I was late, they did a pregnancy test."

He whirled around, unable to believe this. "You found out then and didn't tell me?"

"I wanted to verify it first." Her voice flattened, and resignation settled over her in a thick cloud. "Okay fine, I was scared."

"You lied, told me you were going in for your birth control shot, and I had to find out on RevealPop."

Rising, her eyes flashed and blotches of crimson stained her cheeks. "Like I can control that? Someone stole my medical files. I can't even tell my lover I'm pregnant before some damned tabloid journalist has to get the scoop. Obviously one of the employees in the gynecologist's office tipped them off. I'll go after them, get them fired and prosecute, but the damage is done." Her chest heaved. "Welcome to my life, Hunt, this is it."

Her words from Saturday came flooding back to him. *What I worry is that you can't handle this. My real life.*

He went to the table and scooped up his phone. "Maybe you were right that I can't handle this."

• • •

"You're leaving?" Alyssa couldn't believe how wrong everything had gone.

Hunt stood two feet from her, closed off and coldly angry. "No. I'm going out to clear my head. I don't run, Alyssa. If you're carrying my kid—"

"If?" She sucked in a breath. "I've had two pregnancy tests and an exam. I'm pregnant." Another horrible thought hit her. "Unless you don't think you're the father."

His eyes narrowed. "I just found out and you won't give me a goddamned minute to get my head around it. Fine, you're pregnant and I'm the father. I'll go buy a fucking ring." He turned and crossed the kitchen to the garage door. "Then I'll keep checking the internet to find out the sex of my baby and when it's born."

She'd never seen him like this. His fury blasted over her like frostbite, burning her skin. "Stop it. I'm not trying to trap you into marriage or anything."

With one hand on the door, he stared. "I can understand you needed a day or two to tell me, especially after that picture of you and Eli was released. What I don't understand is lying to my face about the doctor's appointment. I sat out there in the waiting room…" He shook his head. "You didn't trust me. That's what it comes down to. For all your talk of how you're not Rachel, you're not afraid of me, in the moment when you needed to prove it, you took the coward's way out. Now a million people found out before I did. How am I supposed to feel exactly?"

She'd screwed up. "I'm sorry. Please, Hunt, it was a mistake."

"A big one. How do you expect me to handle the fame part of your life if you don't tell me what I need to know? I trusted you with so much…" He sucked in a breath. "I'll be back. Once I calm down, we'll talk. Don't leave the house." He opened the door and left.

Alyssa crumpled into the chair. That look on his face, so cold and remote. Hard.

Unforgiving.

Hot tears splashed down her face. She'd really hurt him. She stared at the door in her kitchen, willing him to come back.

To not leave.

He didn't return. Instead she heard the sound of the garage door rolling shut and his Jeep taking off.

Was he coming back? Would he forgive her?

· · ·

Hunt sat on the blue and white bench on the Malibu pier. A few night fishermen cast their lines, using the lights fixed on the railings to see what they were doing. At the end of the pier, the café was lit up. A few couples strolled along the planks. The waves sounded around the pilings below while his mind churned.

Walking out on Lyssie tonight had been a dick move. He'd known it before he cleared the driveway. A baby. She was pregnant. Why hadn't she been able to tell him? That dug into his chest. Instead, he'd been blindsided by Sienna calling and the RevealPop post of her medical records. Before Lyssie blew back into his life, he'd been fine. Coping. Existing. Nothing really mattered.

Now he had too much to lose. Lyssie meant too much to him, but if she couldn't tell him she was pregnant, then how could they have anything real?

He rubbed a hand over his face. He wanted to be there for her when she was scared, not be the thing she was scared of. He'd been that thing for too long. The Nightmare Ghost Hunter—terrorists and their families, even kids, were taught to be afraid of him. On that final mission when he'd gone after Rand Oliver, Rand had been scared of him. A man who'd once been a friend had seen Hunt and known he was there to kill him, that Hunt would do it if he didn't surrender. Apparently the only thing Rand had been more afraid of than Hunt killing him had been living.

Hunt had told Lyssie tonight he worked for Once A Marine to see the immediate results. True, but he left out the part where he needed to see people happy and relieved he was there to help them. A friend, not the boogeyman. To see that fear in Lyssie's face tonight? She'd been scared of his reaction.

But you walked out. Left her. And what is Lyssie really scared of? Screwing up and not being forgiven.

Dick. Move.

Pulling out his phone, he had to call her, tell her he was on his way home. He had missed calls and tons of texts. No surprise there, the entire world had found out he was going to be a father before he had, but that was something he could work out with Lyssie, not by sitting there brooding. Hunt made the call.

No answer.

The back of his neck tingled, and his instincts pinged off tiny electric sparks of warning. Instantly, he jumped up and jogged to his Jeep.

. . .

Alyssa wished she could put on her headphones and just run, but her knee wasn't quite up to it yet, and it wasn't the best idea to be out alone right now. Instead, she watched one of her mom's old movies, *Cry for Melissa*. That movie had changed her mom's life.

Sitting on the couch, legs drawn up and chin on her knees, she tried to lose herself in the story. Right now, she just wanted her mom any way she could get her, even if it was in a nearly three-decade-old movie.

Next to her on the cushion, her phone vibrated with constant calls, texts and email alerts. She didn't want to talk to anyone but Hunt, but he hadn't called or texted. Total silence. He'd been gone over an hour.

He'll come back. He said he would and he doesn't lie.

Her stomach pitched and burned with regret. Could she and Hunt get past this? They could, right? She heard the distinct sound of the garage door opening. Hunt was back.

Her heart shot into her throat. A mixture of relief, fear and dread popped and boiled, but she was done being a coward. If she had any hope of fixing this, she had to own up to her mistake. Dropping her bare feet to the floor, she clicked off the TV and got up. The house alarm beeped as Hunt came in.

Time to do this. Taking deep breaths, she passed between the end of the couch and the wet bar, and hooked a left to the stairs. Did she have mascara stains on her face from crying? She swiped her fingers under her eyes, and came away with smudges of black on her fingers. Yep, she was a mess.

Stop it. No procrastinating. Grabbing the handrails, she started up.

"Alyssa!"

Oh. Even echoing down the hallway and stairs she recognized Maxine's voice, not Hunt's. That's what she got for not answering her assistant's frantic calls and texts. Maxine knew the guards at the gate, and had a key, garage door opener and alarm codes to her house. "Coming," she called out, halfway up the stairs.

"Do—"

A loud blast reverberated, then a thump.

Alyssa's heart exploded in wild panic. What was that? Should she go up? Or down? She couldn't process—

"Alyssa."

Nate stood at the top of the stairs. Tall, slim and illuminated by the hallway lights, he appeared menacing. At least the gun in his left hand did.

How could he be here, he was supposed to be locked up, and Maxine, he must have shot her. Alyssa twisted around and raced down the stairs. *Get to the phone on the couch. Call for help.*

She hit the floor, spun right and ran hard, diving for the phone.

A heavy weight plowed into her, slamming her over the back of the sofa. It dug into her ribs. Hot pain ripped around her rib cage. She struggled to breathe.

Get the phone. She scrabbled her hand out, reaching toward her sleek cell. The weight on her lifted just as her fingers skimmed the phone. Nate grabbed her ponytail and jerked her back. The phone slid from her grasp as he spun her around to face him. Agony screamed on her left side. Her knees buckled and she dropped to the ground. "Stop. God, stop." Broken rib? Wrapping her arms around herself, she panted.

Nate crouched, the ugly gun in his hand between them.

On her knees, Alyssa forced her eyes up. He had on black slacks and a bloodstained white shirt. Maxine's blood? She almost gagged. Was her friend alive? *Please let her be alive.*

Alyssa had to get away and help Maxine. Focusing on Nate's face, she saw a dark bruise spread over one side, and his lip was cracked and scabbed. That had been from being slammed to the ground after his arrest, she guessed. But his eyes…

Shark eyes. Dark and cold death. Chills raced down her back. A malevolent predator gleamed in their brown depths.

"You're supposed to be in jail." This couldn't be happening.

"I had an emergency fund. I always have a contingency plan, rich girl. Haven't you learned that yet?"

Too calm. Like the man in the elevator threatening her son. "Why?" It came out a desperate plea. "Why me?"

"Because your life should have been mine. You were a tool."

Crazy. Her ribs hurt too much to run. Maybe if she could grasp what he meant, she could figure out a way to get her and Maxine out of this alive. "I don't understand how my life should have been yours."

"Cry for Melissa."

She tried to follow what he meant. "My mom's movie?" The one she'd been watching before she heard the garage door open?

Tightening his hold on her hair, he leaned in, fury darkening his olive skin. "My mom had that role first, but she got pregnant with me and was fired. Your mom got it then. It should have been my mom that became a powerful star."

Insane. This close, the sharp scent of antiseptic and sweat stung her nostrils. Every breath hurt. *If you want to get out of this, think, damn it.* From what Alyssa understood, Nate's mom never got another acting job after she had him. "Is that why you killed her?"

"She was weak. She should have fought for that role, had an abortion."

"You wouldn't be here if she'd had an abortion."

"She had the role of a lifetime and got knocked up. I wasn't letting that happen to us. I made sure, having a vasectomy years ago. We were going to be a real power in Hollywood. I would have attained the life that should have been mine. Now I'll do it another way." Moving suddenly, he grabbed her arm and yanked her up to her feet.

Gasping at the pain, she tried to break free. Panic exploded and she clawed at him. Tried to fight and escape.

He shook her like a ragdoll.

Stabbing pain ripped through her side. Spots danced in her vision as she struggled to breathe. Before she could recover, he dragged her to the sliding glass door. Sick fear swam in her guts and sweat poured down her back.

At the door, he stopped, grabbed her hair, spun her to face it and jammed the gun to her skull. "Open it."

Horror climbed up her throat. "What are you doing?" Her fingers tingled and terror locked her lungs.

"You're going to jump, die on the rocks like you deserve for ruining my life, but the world will think you killed yourself after killing your assistant. It'll be a bigger story than your mom's death. Dragon Wing will produce the movie, making us huge and me, your long suffering ex-fiancé, famous. Wealthy. Powerful."

Hot tears blurred her eyes. "No." *Fight. Run. Escape.* Alyssa tried to spin to the side, to get away.

Nate slammed the heel of his hand into the back of her head. Her forehead bounced off the window. Pain bloomed in sick waves. She heard a crack.

"Open it."

Blinking against her tears and helplessness, she fumbled with the latch. *Don't do it. Fight.* She didn't want to die. She wanted a chance to beg Hunt to forgive her. She loved him and the tiny life just beginning in her. Finally the catch unlatched.

Warm liquid ran down her face, into her eyes. Blood.

Dizziness swirled. *Don't pass out.*

Nate reached around her, shoving open the door and screen.

The pitch-blackness of the night fueled her terror. Death. Five or six steps and he'd force her over the railing. She'd fall into the rocky cliffs.

And die.

She wished she'd told Hunt she loved him.

· · ·

The rollup door to the four-car garage was open, showing Lyssie's blue Mercedes and Maxine's bright yellow Mustang.

Wrong.

The Mustang was parked at an angle with the right front headlight kissing Lyssie's car. Maxine the super-assistant didn't do anything sloppy. In just a few days, he'd caught on to her perfectionism.

Hunt pulled his gun out of the locked glove box in the Jeep and checked it. After sliding out of the car, he went into the garage. Lyssie's security lights showed the fresh blood on the garage floor at the front of the Mustang. There were a few spots on the hood too. Blood spatter.

The car door on the passenger side hung open.

Maxine hadn't come alone. He'd guess she tried to run out of the car and get into the house. Her passenger caught her, hit her and blood spattered.

Madden. It had to be Madden. Fuck. He must have gotten out. For one crazy second, gut-cramping, sweat-popping fear battled his icy control. He jerked his gaze to the door. Lyssie was in there, and most likely in severe danger. He could fail and lose her. That thought chilled his panic.

Training and instinct took over. Pulling out his phone, he texted Coop and Sienna what he knew. They'd call the cops. Hunt had a job to do.

Slipping quietly into the kitchen, he spotted Maxine on the ground. Blood trickled from her nose and lip, staining her skin and coating her blonde hair—she'd taken a punch. Her side bled too. Crouching, he shoved up her shirt to find a ragged gunshot wound. He ripped off his shirt and pressed it to the wound.

Her eyes snapped open and she grabbed his arm. "It's Nate. Downstairs. Hurry."

The words were thick and clumsy. From blood loss? Swollen lip? He didn't know. He met her stare while guiding her hand to the shirt. "Hold this. Stay quiet." Easy to say, hard to do when she had to be in agony. "Paramedics are coming."

A tear slid from her eye.

Hunt was going to kill the bastard who shot her. He had to leave her, had to get to Lyssie.

"Go."

He rose, quickly clearing the main floor despite Maxine telling him they were downstairs. The woman had been in and out of consciousness. He had to do this methodically and carefully. Then he returned and headed into the hallway to the other wing of the house.

Empty.

Halfway down the stairs, he paused where the wall ended and wood railing began. Too quiet. Hunt didn't let himself feel. *Do the job.* Peering around the wall, the rec room was empty, but the slider was open. Moving down the remaining stairs, he scanned the rest of the room. No sign of Lyssie or Madden. He couldn't see into the office, his studio or bathroom, but his attention caught on the sliding glass window, spotting the round spider crack spattered with a few drops of blood. Not good. A second later, he heard a male voice. "Let go."

"Nate! Oh God, don't do this."

Lyssie's shrill, panicked voice unleashed urgency in him. He slid out onto the balcony.

Jesus Christ.

They were at the right corner, where the drop-off was the steepest. Lyssie had somehow climbed over the railing, her toes on the ledge of the balcony, her fingers white-knuckling the round metal railing. One slip, one wrong move…she'd fall to her death.

Blood ran down her face from a gash in her forehead.

Madden stood over her. "Time to die. Let go." The bastard moved the gun from her face, raising it in the air, his intent obvious. He'd slam it on her fingers.

Lyssie screamed, a wrenching sound of building terror.

Hunt rushed forward, praying he could do this. Gun in his right hand, he aimed at Madden's head. He had to do this exactly right. Any mistake and Lyssie died. Both turned to him when he was two feet away. Madden began to slam the gun down.

Don't fail. Hunt fired, and at the same time he shot his left hand out and latched onto Lyssie's left wrist.

She lost her grip on the railing, dropped hard.

The sudden vicious jerk cramped his hand and ripped into his shoulder. He heard a snap. Fuck, his shoulder popped out. *Don't let go!* One look told him Madden was dead. He released his gun and concentrated. Turning, with just enough light coming out of the house, he saw Lyssie hanging over the balcony, only his precarious hold on her keeping her from death.

He caught her other wrist in his right hand. His left arm was losing sensation from the popped shoulder. *Ignore it and hold on.* Relying on his right shoulder, he heaved and tugged, his muscles screaming. Agony burned like a branding iron as he raised her a few inches.

"Get a foot on the ledge." Sweat poured down his face. Below her was total black darkness trying to take her away from him. Focusing on her face, he took in her eyes wide with terror, her skin streaked with blood and tears. Shock, fear, pain, she wasn't quite tracking. "Lyssie, I'm here, baby. I won't let go."

"You came back."

No. He wasn't thinking about how he'd left her right now. *Just get her safe.* "Bend your knees, get your toes on the ledge." His back pulled and burned, pain snapping and popping. His shoulder was a ball of fiery agony. It took all his control to keep calm. He needed her help to gain leverage to pull her over.

Lyssie did it, getting purchase on the ledge with her feet. Relief poured over him. He tugged her up and dragged her over the railing. Sirens blared in the night. His left arm hung useless at his side, but he wrapped his right arm around her shoulders and guided her inside.

"Nate. He's dead. His head…" She shivered violently.

Close-range headshots were brutal and she'd seen it. The horror of it, or the blast of his gun, had shocked her into losing her grip.

Would she look at him as Rachel had? As Rand Oliver had? As so many others who feared him, feared what he truly was?

Chapter Seventeen

Alyssa kept her eyes closed against the lights, praying and waiting. The smells and sounds of the hospital penetrated her private room. Extra guards were posted on the floor to protect her from reporters. She didn't even want to know how the media found out about the attack so quickly.

It was early morning, and misery coated every breath from her bruised ribs. Her head ached thanks to a few stitches and mild concussion. Queasiness came and went.

"Lyssie."

A warm hand landed on her shoulder. She forced her eyes open. Hunt's left arm was in a sling from dislocating his shoulder. Fear for her assistant nearly choked her. "How is she?"

"Maxine's going to make it. They removed her spleen and stopped all the bleeding. She's in recovery and beginning to wake up. Her mom and brother are with her. Doctors are confident she's going to be fine."

"I can't believe it still." They were still piecing together what happened. The police had only been able to ask Maxine a couple questions before she'd gone into surgery, but Nate had bonded out, the police would track that money later. Then he caught Maxine before she got into her condo. Nate had some crazy scheme to kill Maxine then Alyssa and convince the world Alyssa had done it all, even planting those pictures on his computer. They'd really never know the full extent of it since Nate was dead.

"Don't think about it now. Maxine's going to recover. You need rest, Lyssie. I'll come back."

Panic flared. "No. Don't leave me." It was out before she could stop it. Hadn't he done enough? No one could believe that Hunt had simultaneously shot Nate with one hand and caught her with the other. Holding onto her even when his shoulder dislocated. It was impossible. But he'd done it. He hadn't let her fall.

He'd saved her life and she paid him back by trying to hold onto him. *Enough.* Her throat ached but she had to let him go. Maybe he'd choose to be with her, maybe not, but it was his choice. "Sorry. It's okay, go on. Is Cooper here? Can you stay with him or Sienna? You shouldn't be alone with that shoulder." She wanted to be the one to take care of him, but she had to stay overnight in the hospital.

Then what? Go back to her place? Alone?

Alyssa closed her eyes. Tomorrow she'd be up to it. Ready. She had to be. This was her life, and she was going to have a child, one she would love and care for. Hunt would figure out what role he wanted in the baby's life. He wouldn't bail on his child.

The bed dipped, and his hand cupped her cheek. "Lyssie, are you scared? Do you want me to stay with you?"

"Don't ask me that." She whispered it, keeping her eyes shut. "Please, it's okay to leave."

He rubbed his thumb over her cheek. "I'm asking."

"Yes."

Hunt got off the bed, went to her left side. He turned off the overhead light, then slid in and looped his right arm around her, easing her against his side and chest. "I won't leave you. Sleep."

She didn't want to sleep, not yet. Maybe in a month when the memories weren't so overwhelming. His scent and warmth penetrated her cold loneliness, easing her. This was what she needed, the comfort of Hunt, but she had to be fair to him. "I need you right now. I'll be stronger tomorrow. If this is over between us, I'll handle it, I promise."

He didn't say anything.

She was safe with him, even if for a few hours.

"Do you want it to be over?"

Her eyes snapped open. With her hand on his stomach, she felt his tension through the T-shirt he'd acquired somehow. When he'd appeared over that balcony tonight, he'd been bare-chested, his tats gleaming. Soft hospital sounds floated in through the closed door, but all she could feel was Hunt. "No. Why would you think that?"

He exhaled, some of the tension melting in his stomach muscles. "You saw me kill him."

Her eyes stung at the sad, almost resigned words. He thought she would be afraid of him now. "You saved my life. It was a terrible thing to see him shot, Hunt. I'll probably have nightmares." She didn't want to think about it, wasn't ready. She had a tiny fragment of an idea now of why Hunt had repressed so much while doing his job as a sniper. How did someone process that and keep functioning at such a high level of skill? She'd seen up close what he was capable of tonight—extreme speed and precision.

"When I saw you, I was..." The sensation of no matter how bad the moment was, if he was there, it was better. "Suddenly there was hope because my hero was there, the one man who I know I can count on. The one man who I can look into his eyes and feel safe. Even after he had to shoot a man in front of me." She was talking too fast, causing her ribs to hurt, but she wanted to make him understand. "I was grateful. If I didn't live, I'd still have known you cared enough to come back. For once, I was worth coming back for." He hadn't just walked away.

Her mom had left her. Scott had left her. Her stepfather wouldn't even look at her.

Hunt, his parents, and Erin had vanished.

She'd been alone. No one ever came back. Oh, logically, Lyssie understood her mom hadn't wanted to die, that Hunt had been in the Middle East serving his country, and she'd pushed away Erin and her mom, but in her heart she'd felt abandoned and unworthy, as if she were being punished for making mistakes that caused her mom's death.

She admitted her deepest fear. "You came back even after I made a mistake."

"Damn, Lyssie." He stroked her hair. "I should never have walked. I had every right to be pissed, but walking out on you was chicken shit. I realized it pretty quick and was returning."

"Hunt, I'm sorry." She wasn't going to make excuses. She should have told him she was pregnant, not lied about her reason for going to the doctor.

"I know. It wasn't the lie, Lyssie. You were scared to tell

me. I can't deal with that. I need to be the man you run to, not from, when you're scared."

She closed her eyes at the impact of his words. Wasn't that what a relationship was? "Okay. I get it, and for the record, I wasn't scared of you. I was scared of losing you, scared you'd believe I got pregnant on purpose."

"Yeah, I said that, didn't I? Once I had a second to think — I remembered we both forgot the condom that first night we had sex. A child has two parents and both are responsible."

"How do you feel about a baby?"

He was silent for nearly a minute. "I don't know, it's not real yet, but I know that I feel strongly about you. We're not making any decisions right now. It's going to be a rough few weeks as you heal, deal with your feelings about what happened tonight and eventually you'll have to sleep. I'll be there if you're scared."

Of course he knew she was avoiding sleep, so afraid she'd see it again. Being forced over the railing...right up to the point when Hunt appeared. Then shot Nate — that picture was seared into her brain. "How do you do it?"

"What?"

"Live with the memories."

He took a deep breath. "Sculpting helps. It gives me a safe place to vent the emotions. Some of us get professional help, but I couldn't talk about it. At least not then." He paused, gently nudging her face up. "Until you. I've been able to talk to you, and that has made a huge difference."

It was dark in the room, she couldn't really see his eyes, but she could feel the connection between them like a living, breathing thing. "Are you really afraid you'll lose control, hurt someone or worse? Because I don't see it, Hunt. I know

I didn't see it in Nate either—"

"Wrong. You saw it that day in his office and elevator, and then you acted. Before that, I agree, you didn't see it or didn't want to, but once you did, you acted."

That made her feel better, like maybe she'd had a little power over the whole nightmare. It made her feel stronger. "Thank you, but I still don't see it in you."

He was quiet, stroking her hair and cheek, touching her in a way that didn't hurt her ribs but reassured her he was there, that she was safe, giving her exactly what she needed.

"My last mission, I had to kill a man who'd once been a friend. Another sniper. His name was Rand Oliver, and we trained together. Years later, he snapped and killed several other soldiers and support staff, then he vanished. I tracked him. We had to stop him, he was highly trained and extremely dangerous."

She couldn't even imagine. Alyssa turned as much as her ribs allowed, and slid her hand under his shirt to put her palm over his heart. She didn't have any words for him. She wanted to assure him she was there with him, listening.

"He was scared when he saw me. A lot of my targets never saw me, but I let him, hoping he'd surrender. I didn't want to kill him. I just…didn't. Instead, he told me he knew I would do it because they'd turned us into killers. Then he raised his gun at me and it was over in a second."

Oh God. Hunt had done it to save other lives. It's what he'd done his entire Marine career. "And then you came home."

He leaned down, kissing her. "It's taken a long time, baby, but I think I'm finally home. With you. We'll get through these next weeks and months and see where we are. But right now, with you in my arms, I'm home."

Chapter Eighteen

Two weeks later

They went downstairs together. The balcony was gone, and the sliding glass door had been replaced with an arched window and a built-in bench seat. Hunt had had it done, asking Lyssie to trust him. "What do you think?"

Lyssie sat on the cushion that matched her couch, touching the window. "It's beautiful. And safer."

He sat next to her. "I wish I could have taken you home to Sonoma instead of bringing you back here." Lyssie had spotted a little in the hospital, most likely from the trauma. Together with her other injuries, the doctors didn't want her traveling for a full month.

Her face softened. "It doesn't matter where I am, I'm with you. Besides, your parents are here."

Hunt smiled. They'd flown back from Scotland as soon as they'd heard about the attack and set up camp in Alyssa's house to take care of both of them.

Lyssie had been terrified they would be mad at her. As if—she was carrying their grandchild. She truly was a princess in their eyes.

And his.

"They loved your video at the awards dinner last night."

Lyssie couldn't go and Hunt had stayed with her. It had caused a fight between them, Lyssie insisting he had to go until his mom walked in and told her she'd be disappointed in her son if he went. His place was with her while she needed him.

Pleasure danced in her eyes. "I know, both of them have been chatting about it all day today. I gave them copies." She looked around the rec room. "This room has so many happy memories. Nate will never ruin that, but I'm glad the balcony is gone. Thank you."

"I did it for me as much as you. I'd be crazed if you ever went out there again. That memory of you hanging off there will haunt me forever." If he hadn't gotten there in time... He shook it off. They were alive and together.

She took his right hand. Much to his annoyance, his left arm was still in the sling for another week. But his shoulder was healing. "Before you got there that night, I knew I was going to die and I had three regrets. That I'd never see our baby and that I wouldn't get to see Eli when he's an adult if he chooses."

He pushed a lock of her hair back. His mom braided it for her, but pieces always escaped. "That's two, what's the third one?"

She took out her phone and held it up. "I'd like to show you. This is the video I did for you."

He'd forgotten she'd been working on that before the attack. "You want me to watch it now?"

She nodded, pressed play and handed it to him.

The video was her third regret? What, that she hadn't shown him? Didn't matter, this was important to her. Taking the phone, he watched as Lyssie appeared on the screen.

"When I was six years old, I was pretending to be a princess one day. I asked Hunt to be my prince and rescue me from a dungeon. He refused, and told me he wasn't going to be some dumb prince, he was going to be a Marine. I didn't know what a Marine was, but I knew it couldn't possibly be as cool as a prince."

Lyssie smiled into the camera. "Hunter Reece grew up to become a Marine and proved me wrong. This is his story…"

In the next eight minutes, Hunt saw himself through Lyssie's eyes. Images of him growing up, laughing, playing, sculpting, swimming, and then she began interweaving her interviews with him.

His chest hollowed. There were moments where his coldness showed, then melted away to show him laughing and tossing Erin in the pool. There was another shot where he chased and caught Lyssie wearing a tiny bikini, sweeping her up in his arms with a happy grin on his face. Erin must have taken that. How the hell had she done this? There were pictures of him with his friends, Adam, Logan, Griff and Cooper. In all but one, they were having fun.

The grim one was them all standing at attention and saluting Trace Lorrey's casket as it came off the plane. Alyssa panned from that to Hunt's *Sacrifice Remembered* tattoo. The way she did it captured the honor given to those who laid down their lives.

In eight minutes, she had captured Hunt's world. His throat filled as he saw himself through the eyes of Alyssa Brooks.

Lyssie came back on camera. "I know what a Marine is now and it's much better than a prince. A prince is born to a life of privilege, while a Marine is made from courage, strength, honor, sacrifice and vulnerability. They are willing to die so we may live. Hunt is a Marine, an artist, and so much more. He's my hero and the man I've fallen in love with."

The screen faded out as the video ended. The knot in his throat kept growing. This was how she saw him.

Lyssie's eyes shone and her smile tilted in that way that he adored. "That was my third regret, and maybe my biggest, that I hadn't told you I loved you so I'm telling you now. I don't want you to say it back, that's not what this is about." She leaned up and kissed him, then pulled back. "I love you, Hunt. No matter what happens in the future, my love is yours."

He understood she didn't want the words back like a boomerang. She'd given them to him freely. Hunt treasured it, and instead said, "You make me want to be your prince."

• • •

THREE MONTHS LATER

Alyssa laughed when Hunt grabbed her hips as she climbed over the crumbling wall of the castle ruins. "I'm not going to fall." She kept taking pictures, utter joy filling her. Every time she stepped up on a piece of debris, Hunt steadied her. Just as he'd steadied her through the night terrors and emotional days and weeks after Nate's death. His easy patience and constant support had been her lifeline.

Some nights he still sculpted. If she couldn't sleep in bed alone, she went to his studio and curled in the recliner to be near him. He never minded, but covered her up and went back to work, then led her to bed when he was finished.

They'd found peace and friendship together, and for Alyssa, she loved him with every cell of her body. That he'd given her this trip to Scotland took her breath away. "I love this gift, Hunt." On her twenty-fifth birthday, Hunt's present to her had been two tickets to Scotland, and he'd told her he was taking her to the same castle ruins as the one her parents had gotten engaged at.

Being here now, with the cold Scottish winds blowing off the turbulent sea, the jagged stone work that had withstood time and wars, and the incredibly blue sky dotted with clouds, she could almost feel her parents. It had been twenty years since her dad had died, and recalling his physical shape was murky without a picture, but she could recall his voice, the feel of his hands when he scooped her up, his booming laugh and his scent.

And the smile he had whenever he looked at her mom.

The night she almost died she'd thought she might see her mom. She hadn't, but right now, if she squinted, she could see her parents from long ago, her mom sitting on the broken wall, her dad kneeling and asking her to marry him. Tears burned her eyes. "Best gift ever."

Hunt took her hand. "Let's take a break. We've been at this for hours."

"Uh-huh." She was totally on to him. "I'm fine. The second trimester is the best time of pregnancy. No morning sickness, more energy and I'm not too big yet." Except maybe a few hormones that made her cry too easy and laugh too hard. Everything in her life was brighter and richer now. Especially since Maxine had fully recovered and was running Alyssa's life as her assistant.

Hunt straddled a knee-high wall and patted the spot in front of him.

She sat.

He pulled her back to his chest. "This is my first time having a child, so you're going to have to be patient with me. I want to take care of you." He tilted her head back and kissed her. "I also want to get you back to our room, strip off these clothes and lick you until you're begging."

She groaned, knowing full well he could make her beg. The sexy things he said to her did it and he loved wielding his wicked power. "You're taking advantage of my hormones." Hunt loved her changing body.

His rich laughter rippled in her ear. "Hormones, my ass. You want me."

"More every day."

Hunt drew his fingers down her throat, stopping at the top of her jacket. "Same goes."

She knew he wanted her, cared about her. What they were building together was special and it deserved time and care. She wasn't rushing or pushing. The baby would come, and she hoped they'd be married before her first birthday. No matter what, the child would have a mother and father who loved her.

Taking his hand in hers, she stared out over the rugged landscape. "I wanted to ask you something." Linking their fingers, she asked, "Are you sure about leaving Once A Marine?"

"Were you sure about giving up Dragon Wing to Parker?"

"Ninety percent." She didn't regret it. She and Parker talked a few times, but it was always business. She didn't have a real relationship with him, but her mother and Parker had loved each other. She didn't want Dragon Wing, and so she gave him her shares in her mother's memory.

"I'm ninety-one percent. Once A Marine helped me transition from active Marine to civilian. I loved the work, but it's time to lay down my gun. I did my job to my country, now I'm going to focus on my personal life. The only people I want to protect from here on in are my family and friends."

Alyssa took a breath, relaxing against him. He may have been right that she needed to take a break from all the walking and climbing. She saw no reason to admit that to him, though. "And you want to sculpt."

He wasn't ready to publically show his pieces yet. His art had taken on a very personal meaning to him. They were his healing. When he'd been ready, he'd shown her all the sculptures in his studio in Sonoma. They were stunning. Some were tragic but some were surprisingly tender, showing the heroism that happened daily on the fields of war. All of them had an emotional brilliance that hadn't been in his early work.

"Yes." He laid his free hand on her belly over her coat. "I'm much more interested in taking care of my family."

She couldn't help but smile, seeing his hand over her stomach. "You mean your daughter." He'd been excited to find out they were having a girl.

Hunt got up, moved around to straddle the wall, facing her. "I mean you. You're the woman I love, Lyssie, the woman I want to spend the rest of my life with. I can't ask your father for your hand, so instead I brought you here to the place your parents got engaged."

Ask her father for her hand? Alyssa's heart sped up, her head buzzed. He was asking her to marry him? Her entire body flooded with a want so powerful, tears filled her eyes. "You love me?" He hadn't said it before now.

He leaned his forehead against hers. "I wanted to bring you here, to a place where you can share this memory with that of your parents. I love you, Lyssie. I was pretty damn sure of it the night I caught you before you fell off the balcony. Holding you there, in that moment, I knew I'd go over with you before I let you go."

Her chest hollowed and she believed him. What he'd done that night had been superhuman. "I love you, too."

He smiled. "Yes, you do. You love all of me, even the part of me that killed a man in front of your face. When you had nightmares you turned into my arms, not away, do you know what that trust feels like?"

"Like showing me your art you kept locked up. A trust you will die before you betray."

"Exactly." With his head pressed to hers, his breath fanning gently over her face, Hunt added, "When I ask you this, you need to know I'm asking you as my friend and lover, not the mother of my child. Because our child has us whether or not we're married. Are we clear?"

How was it that out on these windswept ruins in a vast open space, they were shrouded in warm intimacy and Alyssa could swear her parents were holding hands and looking on? That they would give their blessing? She trembled, afraid to believe she could have this much happiness. "Yes."

Rising again, he pulled a small box out of his jacket

pocket. Hunt knelt and took her hand. "I told you three months ago, when I'm with you, I feel as if I'm finally home. I love you Alyssa Marie Brooks. Will you marry me?" In his other hand, he snapped open the box and held it up.

The sun glinted off the ring, but Alyssa stared only into Hunt's eyes. Those beautiful eyes made of the lightest blue and deepest love. The sensation of her parents faded away.

Right there in front of her was her future, her home and her family.

"Yes."

Acknowledgments

Thank you to Alethea Spiridon Hopson for your support, editing and patience as we worked on the Once A Marine series. I appreciate all your guidance and suggestions whenever I lost my way in a story. In particular, I'd like to thank Alethea for supporting Alyssa's story of a young mother who chose to give her baby up for adoption. That takes a special kind of bravery and love, and I'm grateful to have had the opportunity to share that in this book.

Thank you to my husband, Dan Apodaca. You are my hero every single day.

A special thank you to Marianne Donley for jumping in to help me when I hit the wall and panicked while writing this book.

And to all my friends and family, thank you for not giving up on me when a book pulls under and I fall short of being the wife, mom, sister or friend that you deserve. I know I say this after I finish every single book, but I'll try harder!

No really, I will…okay, we all know I'll end up being Crazy, Stressed Jen all over again with the next book. But I count myself a very lucky woman to have you all in my life.

And most important of all, Thank You Readers! You're the reason I go to my keyboard every day. I can write the words, but it's in your hearts and minds that the characters truly come alive. Thank you for sharing your time and love with the characters in my books!

About the Author

Award-winning author Jennifer Apodaca grew up in Southern California and met her very own hero at the dog pound. She worked there, he came in on business, and it was puppy love. They married and had three wonderful sons.

While her husband worked on his master's degree, Jen did the mom thing by day and went to college at night with the intention of pursuing a marketing degree. But her true passion was writing. With time at a premium, she had to make a choice.

Choosing writing, she poured herself into her dream. A mere eight years later, she published her first book, Dating Can Be Murder. In her career, Jen has written a fun and sexy mystery series, a variety of contemporary romances, and a dark, sizzling paranormal series under the name of Jennifer Lyon.

Jen has achieved many of her dreams except for attaining a self-cleaning house, a latte delivery service, and finding the holy grail of non-fattening wine and chocolate. She can live with those disappointments as long as she can keep writing the stories she loves to share with readers.

Find out more about Jen at www.jenniferapodaca.com or https://www.facebook.com/jenniferlyonbooks

Discover the **Once a Marine** *series…*

THE BABY BARGAIN

Former Marine, Adam Waters keeps his heart on ice, even with the one woman he can't forget, hometown girl, Megan Young. But when Adam learns the shocking truth that Megan's child is really his, will his heart thaw or turn to stone?

HER TEMPORARY HERO

Wealthy, sexy, and emotionally haunted Logan Knight needs a temporary wife. Enter former beauty queen Becky Holmes. She and her baby are on the run from her dangerous ex and she'll do anything to protect her child…even agree to a sham marriage if it means protection. But Becky and her baby trigger Logan's darkest memories. While he tries to keep his distance, he can't. His attempt to have it all backfires into a betrayal that forces Becky into a heart-wrenching choice no woman should ever have to make.

CPSIA information can be obtained
at www.ICGtesting.com
Printed in the USA
LVOW03s0813040318
568589LV00001B/34/P